Treatment

Also by A. C. H. Smith

Fiction
The Crowd
Zero Summer

Non-fiction
Orghast at Persepolis
Paper Voices

a novel by A.C.H. Smith

Treatment

Weidenfeld and Nicolson London

The author acknowledges assistance from the Arts
Council of Great Britain.

ISBN 0 297 77073 x

Setting by
TRI-AM Photoset Ltd
Bridge Foot, Warrington
Printed in Great Britain by
Morrison & Gibb Ltd
Tanfield, Edinburgh

We have more moral, political, and historical wisdom than we know how to reduce into practice.

P. B. SHELLEY

If with this brush one composes poems and essays, and writes characters, and people look at the result and feel no ache, no itch, nothing at all, one might as well break one's arm. What use is it?

LU CH'AI

Similia similibus curantur.

The stanzas from W. H. Auden's 'Many Happy Returns' are quoted by kind permission of Faber and Faber Ltd., publishers of his *Collected Shorter Poems 1927-57*; and the lines from Robert Graves's 'Leda' are quoted by kind permission of Cassell & Co. Ltd., publishers of his *Collected Poems*.

One

It's hard to remember what happened first, or next. Events will reorder themselves as cogs or chains to prove your story the right one. (I avoid such phrases as: the true one, the real one, or – Lord save us – the honest one. I'll stick to right, a word by now sucked bloodless by the trained vampires in advertising agencies.) Whether Lise deWitt ('my paternal grandfather came over from Rotterdam' is how she explains her name, and adds, if pressed, or impressed, 'with a suitcase full of gin') was pregnant by her lawful husband, Andrew Rengard, before or only after they met Martin Shy is not, probably, something they could be sure of themselves. Around that time, it was, anyway. Because by the time Martin had proposed to them that he should make a film about them, and they had been flattered, as anyone might be, then suspicious, then reassured, contracted, witnessed and paid half in advance, £150, then recorded on tape and booked for the first day of filming, Lise was definitely going to have a baby. She hasn't had it yet.

'Why us?' one of them, Lise or Andrew, asked Martin, between being flattered and suspicious.

'It's one of a series about starting,' Martin answered. 'You are starting to be actors, at the drama school. Other programmes in the series will be taking a look at a couple of lads who are starting to be footballers, a girl who's starting to be a lawyer, a feller who's starting to be a tea-taster, and there's – what else have we got lined up, Julia?'

9

Julia, the PA, was starting to tell him, but Martin went on, 'It's not a vocational series, though. We shan't be brilliantly interested in the actual jobs, prospects, training, anything like that. It's not one of those mid-afternoon ghettoes, but prime time, 8.30 in the evening. It's the concept of starting, the psychological gearing-up to growth, and change, and leaving the nest, that we're interested in. It's about people, not jobs.'

'But people are about jobs, don't you think?' Andrew asked him. 'Psychology is a function of the conditions of production.'

'I'd agree,' Martin answered, 'up to a point. We can take that up on the wildtrack, perhaps. But the point I'm making now is that you are starters in another sense, too. You're starting to be married. When was it?'

'February,' Lise said.

'Right,' Martin agreed. 'And there's another thing. In your case there's a built-in extra for us, because one day one of you, or both, just might make it to the top in acting. And in that happy event we would be happy, too, to have some archive film of you in your starting days. In that sense, for us it's an investment. So you see, you're naturals. The Head of Programmes thinks so, too. He wants to meet you.'

'But why us?' one of them wanted to know. 'There are other married people at the drama school.'

'But not a married couple,' Martin said, 'not according to our researcher.'

'There's two who are going to get married.'

'God bless them,' Martin said. 'Well, not to pussy-foot with you, you both happen to be very good looking, and that is never a disadvantage on television.'

In television it is a different matter, you could guess from taking a look at Martin. His face is one of those that would be left over when you had sorted the rest of the pack into suits. Not ugly, not handsome, not youthful nor

10

aging, not intellectual nor daft, nor chunky or rounded or revoltingly disfigured by an acid-thrower. The eyes are grey-blue and calm, slightly hooded, a feature emphasised when he leans forward, as he does habitually when making a point, and touches or holds some part of you, your foot if you are seated cross-legged, as though he trusts touch to focus the other senses. His hair, that thinly veils his ears, is on the fair side of mouse, the smile on the small mouth rare. His best friends, of whom he has many, would concur in calling his an alert face, touched with scepticism. When he is shy, conforming to his surname, as he was at first with Lise and Andrew, he is good at playing the boorish television director, and enjoys it. He enjoys any mask, on himself or another. 'I have an anonymous face,' he says. 'People never remember they've met me before. It's my most valuable professional asset. I am invisible.'

'It's what Keats calls "negative capability" you mean,' Lise told him, 'your receptivity to your subjects.' And she smiled, to apologise for so many syllables, although most of them were John Keats's fault. Lise's smile serves her much as Martin's touch serves him, to confide that, behind all this fiddle with words, one understands another. She had learned to smile as a child, along with her elder brother and younger sister, children of a successful barrister, now a successful judge, and of a mother, Lady deWitt, commonly admired as 'a remarkable woman'. Lise has inherited little of her mother's force; but from her father she learned to adore dressing-up and acting, and her wide mouth and eyes, short nose and blonde hair testify that the surname is not the only Dutch attribute handed down to her. She is a sweet peach, all right, and her mother was speaking the truth when she told Lise that a girl with her looks could have as many suitors as she chose, so why was she rushing into marriage only halfway through her drama course,

11

with a man she had known barely twelve months. 'You haven't got to, have you, darling? Because, you know. . . .'

'Yes, mother, I have got to, but not for the reason you're thinking of.' And with a similar obstinacy, practised against her mother's force, Lise insisted that the wedding would not be in church, much as she would have loved the bridal dressing-up. Andrew had set his face against it, his dark, Celtic face that had prayed to the Protestant God every day of his childhood, facing his father's face or next to it in a pew, but would pray no more. His faith had left him, been driven from him by the equally stern catechism of Karl Marx. Andrew's sternness was one of the reasons why Lise had got to marry him, and did, although as an actor she retained her maiden surname.

'And your maiden ways,' Andrew teased her. She was cooking. The pages of Elizabeth David, open in front of her where she worked, were translucent with greasy stains. Every knife or plate she took was another fresh one, and the dirties would have filled the sink but for Andrew, washing them up and putting them away, often for Lise to use again in five minutes. He loved to see her cooking for them in their kitchen, but wondered if creation had to be so profuse.

She took no notice of his teasing. Her mind was on the film, on what she could find to say when millions of people were listening. 'It's simply no good Martin telling me just to talk naturally,' she said. 'There's no such thing as talking naturally. You always talk *to* someone, don't you?'

'Don't let it get to you,' Andrew told her. 'I'm not.'

'It's all right for you. You're good at putting ideas together.'

'And television is marvellous at putting them asunder again, especially if they threaten to breed doubts in the minds of whoever might be watching. I'm interested

12

simply in seeing how much they'll let me get across, and where the Tilt light will flash on.'

Lise just shook her head, and went on slicing onions.

'If you let it get to you,' Andrew told her, 'if you rate your own performance by their scales of what makes successful television, you're lost. You're lost. You've got to treat the whole thing as an experiment. But the subject of the experiment isn't you. It's television.' He put his arms around her waist.

'You may be right – '

'What is this "may be"?' He nuzzled her neck.

'—but it doesn't solve the problem of what I am going to say down the microphone.'

'Look, I'm not having you lose a minute of sleep about it. It's not too late to pull out, if you'd rather.'

'No. That would be shirking a challenge.'

'I can see the case for having nothing to do with it. With any of television. It's just a mystification, the way it's used by the structures of power in our society.' Andrew sat down, and gazed at the waste-bin. 'But there is a case, also, for getting inside the structure and learning more about it, so that you're better equipped to work for change in it, when the time comes.'

Lise put the daube in the oven. 'Will you tell me when that's been in for four hours?' she asked.

Andrew looked moodily at his watch.

She took off her apron, and smiled at him. 'O come on, sweetheart,' she said, 'it's not as serious as that. I suppose I'll manage somehow.'

Stern is what Andrew's face was, some weeks later, when he read through the dossier that now follows.

Memo

From Martin Shy
Subject STARTERS: Lise deWitt and Andrew Rengard
To Head of Programmes

Attached find the transcripts of the tapes I have recorded in the sound studio for use on wildtrack.

I have underlined the passages I expect to use. We have already spoken about the problems. You will see for yourself.

As I suggested, I hope a balance can be restored in the filming by concentrating visually on Lise, even when it is Andrew's over-articulate thoughts we are hearing on wildtrack. So that we place him as a condition of her life.

It may be that Lise will give away more of herself on film. We shall see when we start next week.

Encs.

Printer – italics
where underlined, please

MARTIN SHY: Start by telling me why you're at drama school.

ANDREW RENGARD: I'm there because it's my modest ambition to change the world. Or at least the society I live in.

MS: Go on.

AR: To change the world it is necessary to change people. When someone says human nature never changes, it is bad faith speaking. I believe that it is necessary to subvert bad faith on the social level, from which all the other changes, in the psyche and so on, will come. We, *as actors we can show people alternative ways of enacting what they really are, alternative ways of relating to other people*, without bad faith, with generosity, because they recognise other people's own human needs, and weaknesses. And their strengths, too. And their own. I'm talking about reciprocal exchange. That's what society is, isn't it? *That's where we get our self-definitions from, or should do, from what we give and get, not what we have.* We need much less than we have, and much more, much more between us, shared. And I believe, with Peter Brook, that it is in the theatre that the charge can be generated among a circle of people sharing something, a community, the audience, that might switch all their circuits over to. . . . I'm sorry, I'd better jump off that sentence before it carries me round another time. Can we stop the tape?

MS: There's no need. Don't worry. We can use as much tape as we like.

AR: When I get on a high golden horse like that, going up and down, round and round, and the organ playing, you know, it can start sounding facile, and I get dizzy, I want to throw up. What about the recordist through there? Don't tell me we can use as much of him as we like, or you'll embarrass me.

MS: John's not worried, are you?

AR: I do believe the Peter Brook bit, mind you. I believe everything I said, or tried to say. It just sounds so pat, sitting here in a comfortable chair with only you to say it to.

MS: Sitting here in my comfortable chair.

AR: Right.

MS: But when it goes out, it goes out to people sitting in their comfortable chairs. So just talk to me. Interest me. Don't worry if you get something wrong. We can take care of the sincerity later, when we edit. Tell me, did you always intend to be an actor?

AR: No, not till I decided to come to the school. I was – what? – twenty-five then. Most of the others there aren't over twenty. At their age I was at a university.

MS: What were you studying?

AR: Classics. But *I quit after two terms. I realised that*

15

what I was doing was preparing for entrance exams to the upper class. All through school I'd been a bright kid, you see, and the headmaster there was a talent scout for capitalism, like most of them, so he kept telling my father that I had a brilliant academic career coming to me. And my father drank it all in, and it sounded wonderful to him, because, you know, he'd left school at fourteen and never had the chances, and all that. And although he's been a socialist all his life, he's kept on the right side of God, just in case. He's a sidesman in the local church, for Christ's sake. So he didn't really ever rumble the political score in my brilliant academic future, and nor did I. *Until I went to university I'd never asked myself a serious question. As soon as I got there, there were suddenly a lot of questions, all of them serious, and the answer to every one of them was the same, get out. So I did.*

MS: How did your parents take it?

AR: *My father still can't understand it.* I explain it to him, but he always comes back to quoting Anthony Crosland at me, about equal opportunities, and all the other lies. *And I can't really get to him, because at the same time I gave up Christianity, and that went in deeper still, you know.* Because I did that, stopped believing, and there's no explaining that, he doesn't really pay any attention to what I tell him about politics. It's been rough for him.

MS: You feel guilty about that.

AR: No, not guilty. I haven't betrayed anything I believe in. Just remorseful, that I had to do it to him. Rather brutally disappointed the aspirations he had for me. *It's sad. I'm the only child, you see, and my mother died when I was still a baby, so my father's not got a great deal else to build on.* Maybe I'll get to play the great Shakespearean leads at Stratford yet, and make it up to him that way.

MS: Is that what you're aiming at – Stratford?

AR: I don't honestly think so. I'm not sure. I'd rather do

16

that than be some Professor of Greek, certainly, but I think it's another class rip-off, really. Let me tell you something. *I saw my old headmaster about two months ago.* We hadn't met since I quit university. I was at home, seeing my father, and we went for a walk together by the river, and there he was, taking his dog for a walk, still the local headmaster, still holding out this awful limp hand, that you have to move up and down like a housewife sussing out a lump of cod. He'd heard what had happened, of course, but I hadn't seen him in six years. And he came on so bloody patronising, about treading the boards, and all that brand of shit. Oh, sorry, I can't say words like that on television, can I?

MS: Not in prime time. But don't worry, we'll edit it out.

AR: What really got up my nostrils was that he was exploiting the situation. He knew that with my father there I wasn't going to urge him to get stuffed. My father's got to go on living in that place. *And after he'd twisted his twills with patronising me, he talked across me to my father, about how he himself had had to slave away night after night at Greek verbs when he was young, but I'd been a natural, mastered it all effortlessly—'iffortlessly' he pronounces it—only to throw it away after two terms at the university, but he supposed that I knew what I was doing, and that one day he and my father would be sitting in the stalls clapping my rendition—'rendition' for Christ's sake—of Hamlet at Stratford.* I should be so lucky, I was thinking. And it made me wonder about Stratford, that did, I mean about all that big-deal theatre scene. The funny thing was that he was doing the most knock-out audition piece for Polonius, if he'd only realised it. *My poor old father of course was just nodding his head, and saying 'Tsk-tsk, well, you know,' because the headmaster represents the imperialism of brains, you see, and my father belongs to one of the subject tribes in that field. I suppose, if I'm honest, I was squirming partly*

17

at the memory of how I'd been eager to please that man when I was at school, how beautifully he'd kept my eyes shut to the realities of the situation at that school, kept all of our eyes shut, with his calculated drip-feed of approval. I have to admit that the work I did at school, the good academic work, I did so as not to disappoint that man. I was on a real teacher-pleasing trip for about four years. Wow. I got the shudders on when I thought how it would be now, if I'd gone through the degree course and come out with brilliant honours, and went into some university post, and went back there now, and met that man, and I'd have had to stand there being the paragon of all the false faiths he lays on the kids there. It gave me ideas of going to the school one afternoon, walking into his sixth-form classics class, and telling them the way it really is, in front of him, the education rip-off that people like him are perpetrating on the working class, which almost all the kids there come from, or they're petit-bourgeois, it's much the same, just one generation on, usually.

MS: What did you say, in fact – anything?

AR: Not really, with my father there. I thought when he wasn't looking I'd kick his spaniel, but I didn't get the chance. I just said, when he was going, 'Mind that souped-up Pekinese doesn't bolt with you.' Thin smile, with the corners of his mouth, like that.

MS: What happened after you left university?

AR: *For three or four years I knocked around doing all sorts of things. I had no particular aim. I was on the buildings, I washed dishes, worked on a farm in France for about six months, threw crates around in a brewery, things like that. I spent all the time I could reading.* Marx, Engels, Herzen, Lenin, Rousseau, Shelley, Alex Comfort, Laing, Cooper, Reich, Lawrence, Berger, Raymond Williams. The following week. . . . No, I really made up for all the years I'd wasted. And *I suppose I might have gone on like that indefinitely, but then I read a book about*

18

Peter Brook, and I got really interested in what people like him and Grotowski are doing, and I thought maybe this just might be a way of returning to society the things I'd learned from all the other reading I'd done. *So I found out about drama schools, and this one took me.*

MS: Why did you think it necessary to go through a drama school? I mean, there are plenty of community theatre groups where you wouldn't need a formal training.

AR: Yes, but quite honestly most of them are just jerking off, most that I've seen. They've got enthusiasm and social concern and the desire to express themselves and awaken people, but it isn't enough. The kind of actors Brook and the others are using have got to be trained instruments. *I didn't know the first thing about how to use my body, or my voice. When you do know about such things, you've got so much more power*, as an instrument. You know, one inflection in the voice, if it's the right one, can communicate something that six pages of tirade, or lament, or whatever, couldn't get near. *For me, theatre is a political act, and when you're into politics you're into power*, whatever kind of power is appropriate to your aims. So I want to learn as much as I can about the power of this instrument, myself. Then use it.

MS: How are we for tape, John? [. . .] No, thanks. Let's wrap it up for today. Okay?

AR: Fine by me.

[TAPE ENDS]

MARTIN SHY: When did you decide you wanted to be an actor?

LISE deWITT: Oh, I've always wanted to act, all my life.

MS: Is it possible to say why?

L dew: I suppose it started when I was little. *My parents used to take us to the theatre quite often, not just to pantomimes but to other things as well, musicals, opera even. And Shakespeare, quite often, and other plays that most*

19

people would think were just for grown-ups. I used to love it, everything about it, and I knew it was what I wanted to do.

MS: Was it just that your parents loved theatregoing, or did they perhaps want to encourage you to be an actor?

L dew: Oh, I don't think they specially wanted to encourage me. I mean, they always took the three of us, my brother and sister as well, and, well, my brother anyway has no ideas about acting. He's a lawyer, like my father, only a company lawyer. I think my sister might want to act, but she's only sixteen at the moment. No, *they are quite pleased now, I think, that I'm doing it, but they didn't plan it for me, or anything*.

MS: Your father is a judge, I know, and before that he must have been a barrister. There's a lot of acting in that, don't you think?

L dew: Oh, he wouldn't deny it.

MS: But what I'm getting at is that possibly your desire to act comes from there, also. Did you watch him perform in court, often?

L dew: Hardly ever. Only twice in my life, I think.

MS: Why?

L dew: Well, it's not the sort of performance that you want spectators at, is it? Especially not your own children.

MS: Go on.

L dew: Well, I suppose – I mean, it is a performance, right, but it's only for the court's sake, not a show for the public. Justice has to be enacted, and seen to be enacted.

MS: But not seen by the populace in whose name the justice is done?

L dew: Not by one's own children, necessarily. That's all I mean. Of course you've got to have a public gallery, but it's for people who are interested in justice being done, isn't it, not who are interested in the performers? But, going back to what you were saying, yes, *I suppose it's true that knowing my father's job entailed dressing-up and*

20

performing in public probably did have some effect on my feeling about acting. I always used to read the *Times* law reports when he was in a case there. 'I see you're reading my script again,' he'd say, when he saw me. We always did a lot of dressing-up and doing our own plays at home, when we were little. My brother Ben usually wrote them, and directed them, I was the hero, and my younger sister was the heroine, and my brother would be the villain. I remember we did an opera, once. All the tunes were Beatles songs, but we put new words to them.

MS: No doubt your father wouldn't have wanted you to hear some of the things that come out in court.

L dew: I suppose not, no.

MS: You sound as though that's something you'd never thought about before.

L dew: I don't think we were over-protected as children, if that's what you're getting at. We were never forbidden to watch anything on television, for instance, and you see things there that are just as bad as anything you might hear in a courtroom. Worse, very often. You don't get children burned by napalm in court, at least.

MS: I'd guess you had a very happy childhood.

L dew: I did, yes. I'm grateful for it.

MS: Grateful to your parents?

L dew: Yes. Who else?

MS: You might feel grateful to the system that allowed your parents to create that happy childhood for you.

L dew: What system do you mean?

MS: When I talked to Andrew yesterday, he was very lucid about the education system, and how that is one part of a larger system, which I imagine he would define as capitalism. I can't believe you haven't talked about all that with him.

L dew: Oh sure, we've talked a lot about the class structure, and we both recognise that I was brought up in a relatively privileged area of it.

21

MS: To which you feel grateful.

L dew: Yes. I can't pretend I didn't have a happy childhood, and I can't turn round now and say I wish I hadn't, can I? It's happened, and it's finished.

MS: Is it?

L dew: For me, it is.

MS: But would you now, knowing what you know, want to criticise that system at all?

L dew: No. I've told you. I hate the attitude that because there is misery in the world one has no right to be happy. I'd like to try and help more kids have as happy a childhood as I did. That's what I feel.

MS: Will acting help you to do that?

L dew: It could.

MS: How?

L dew: I don't know, exactly. I just think – well, I might do theatre-in-education work, in schools. That's one possibility. At the moment, I'm too busy learning to be an actor to think it all through, about the applications of what I'm doing.

MS: You've told me why you always wanted to act. But can you say why you still want to act, now?

L dew: *All the people I've ever passionately envied have been actresses. Vanessa Redgrave, Dorothy Tutin, Edwige Feuillère, Anna Karina, Joanne Woodward.... Oh, I don't know, watching people like that has given me an obsession, I suppose it is, with wanting to do what I've seen them do, when they have moved me more than anything else can. I know I can do it,* but I've got to work and work at it. But I love the work, at the school.

MS: Where does getting married fit in to that?

L dew: It doesn't fit in to that. I just happened to meet a feller I fell in love with, so we got married. It's got nothing to do with my acting, except that of course we often work together, in classes, and that's nice, because there's a trust

22

there. And we can help each other, with technical things, and so on.

MS: Andrew talked about what Peter Brook means to him. Does he mean the same to you?

L dew: Sort of. Well, not quite the same. I mean, it would be fantastic to work with Brook, because of what he does for an actor. Everybody says so. Did you see the *Dream*? I went four times. I would have given anything to be in that. But – well, right.

MS: Go on.

L dew: Well, I was just going to say that Andrew's into a slightly different thing about Brook. He gave me that book to read, you know, about all the experimental work, and it's fascinating, of course, but parts of it seem a bit weird to me, really, and I'm not sure I'm all that interested in that aspect.

MS: What aspect, exactly?

L dew: Experiments with language, and that kind of thing. It's obviously fascinating for the actors who are doing it, but I don't think it's quite what I need, at the moment, anyway. Later on, perhaps.

MS: Does Andrew try to get you interested in that aspect?

L dew: In Brook's experiments, do you mean?

MS: And the idea of bringing a community together with an act of theatre.

L dew: Well, any act of theatre does that, if it's good enough, don't you think?

MS: Maybe. But what I think isn't going out on television. I want to hear what you think.

L dew: I'm not marvellous at thinking aloud, I'm afraid. Andrew is, I know. I have to let things work themselves out, inside my head. I'm sorry, I suppose most of what I've said isn't much use to you for the programme, is it? It's so amazingly easy to forget that it's going to go on television, when it's just you and me sitting here.

MS: Good.

L dew: Why good?

MS: Because that's what television is, just one or two people sitting in a room. The millions of viewers don't aggregate into the sum of their parts. There's no such thing as a mass audience, in fact, for television. There's no crowd response, no dynamic of numbers, like you get at Wembley, or indeed in a theatre. The mass audience is in fact millions of tiny, separate audiences, with no way of hearing what all the other millions are thinking of the programme, so they all react separately. More honestly. If you bear that in mind, it might help you not to feel shy.

L dew: I don't feel shy.

MS: Let's wrap it up there for today. Thank you, John.

[TAPE ENDS]

MARTIN SHY: This time I'd like you to talk about the other sense in which you and Lise are starters, in your marriage. Could you, perhaps, describe Lise as you see her?

ANDREW RENGARD: *She's beautiful. That's the first, superficial thing. She's a bit mixed up in her head.* I gather something of that came out when you were talking to her in here, yesterday.

MS: I hope I didn't make her upset.

AR: She was a bit upset at herself. Not at you. *I find it touching, that mixed up, lovely head of hers. And the spirit in her that is determined to get it all straight, eventually. She's got so much energy—courage, if you like. And she is utterly English, in some way.*

MS: Can you say in what way?

AR: I haven't quite got it figured out myself, yet. *I'm still trying to separate the Englishness from the upper-classness.* For myself, and then, I hope, for her. It's an insight that could help her a lot, when I've got it to offer her. But the BBC-Oxford voice has implanted in all of us

24

so deep an identification of Englishness with upper-classness that it takes a lot of work to unpeel one from the other. It's something to do with her spirit. It would still be utterly English, no matter if she talked like Garbo. But then, she couldn't. The voice is the character. I will admit – since this studio seems to be some kind of admissions ward – that the first few times we – what am I allowed to say on television? – made love, there was a not entirely honourable. . . . I'm sorry, that sentence has got away from me, let me take another shot at it. *It wasn't just Lise's beauty that turned me on, and the affection we already had for each other, but also there was an extra hit in it for me from her class.* I realise that's not a very flattering thing to say about myself, or about Lise either, but it's something we've talked about, and recognise now. Making love to a judge's daughter was politically erotic. Yes. At last – you'll have to edit the tape, but I want to say it to you – at last I could say 'Fuck the ruling class' and really mean it. I'd put flesh on the phrase. Right, resume after that edit. I'd never taken such expensive clothes off a girl's body before. It was very powerful, symbolically: under the class layers was simply the thing she is. And when we made it at her parents' place, it got almost ritualistic, on the velvet upholstery, our feet bare on absurd little extravagances, like Persian rugs, or whatever, worth several hundred quid. I used to find myself humming that old Peter Sarstedt number, Where Do You Go To, My Lovely? – you remember? I'd never been in a house like that. Incredible. Even in the lavatory, when they'd been just before me, the smell of their shit was sweeter than you get in any ordinary house. I'd better stop, before it gets to be one long edit.

MS: How do you, with the views you hold, get on with Lise's parents?

AR: They know what I think, and they know I know what they think, and we manage to contain it within a kind of ironic humour towards each other. It's a bit edgy. Quite stimulating, really. Obviously they didn't trust me at first, and probably still don't. There was one immortal moment when her mother – not her father – said to me, 'Look, there is something we have got to ask you, Andrew, and I'm afraid I can't find any way of putting it except to say, "are your intentions, honourable?"' It was a gift. 'You mean, I have a choice?' I answered. When you're into plagiarism, why settle for anything but the best? That same night, I remember, I had a dream. I was staying at their house, and what I dreamed was that it was our wedding day, and it was all in morning suits and so on – though in fact we'd already said we wanted to get wed in the register office – and I simply could not obtain a grey silk tie anywhere, and I felt terrible about it. And the whole affair was gloomy, everyone was very down about it all, including ourselves. Fantastic gloom all round. And then, later on in the same dream, we'd been married for two days and I suddenly realised that I'd simply forgotten to sleep with Lise both nights. Just overlooked it.

MS: Do you have an attitude to sexuality, I mean a view about it, which links with the rest of the political views, and so on, that you hold?

AR: Do I? How much tape have we got?

MS: No problem.

AR: Well, I'll keep it as terse as I can. I'd better start by emphasising that *I had an extremely puritanical upbringing*. I don't just mean strict – though it was strict – but puritanical in the much better sense in which Richard Hoggart called Lawrence a puritan in the Lady Chatterley trial, years ago. I think it has to do with a kind of economy of sexuality, or ecology, even – the argument that sex is healthy only if it be contained, balanced, within some larger pattern of meaning. So that promiscuity, or masturbation, which is much the same thing, is wrong, bad for you, not because teacher says so but because it offends the

26

natural pattern, the proper place of sexuality in nature. Sex becomes an end, not a means. That's the definition of puritanical I mean: a loathing of anything gratuitous. That kind of sexuality is merely self-gratifying, and so it serves merely to drive you inside your own skin. It's what Lawrence calls 'personal sex'. It's sterile, literally – nothing grows from it. Perhaps it's just hindsight, but I think I knew that, really, even before I read Lawrence. Maybe it's one of the few pieces of valuable knowledge that I got from a strict Christian upbringing. It really was puritanical. My father and I said prayers together at home every morning, on our knees, hands together. I think that's unusual. I'd say it was more rabbinical than Protestant, nowadays. And I dressed very soberly. I still do, as you've seen. It's not conventional what I wear now, no smart suits or ties, but I've never felt any desire to break out into flower-power gear, for instance. Trendy vicars I find obscene, really I do. Come the revolution, pow! pow!, up against the wall. They'll be the very first to go, even before the generals. Because they're more to blame. So it was a puritanical upbringing in that sense, and also in a reverence for study, working hard at one's calling, which in my case was the Classics. Though of course there was the worse sort of puritanism in it too, that eternal hammering at sin, and failure, and our unworthiness in the eyes of the all-judging Lord. We are all in His debt, and can never pay off the instalments. It is a religion of lament, you know, Christianity, more so than Islam, I think. And a religion of suffering, and cruelty. That omnipresent nailed-up man. What other religion presents you with a central image of torture? And celebrates it with a thinly disguised ritual of cannibalism? When they talk of original sin, what they really mean is original guilt. If I could ever believe in Christianity again, it would have to be through some radically different sacrament, one that started in terror, and then atomisation of the self, and then

healing and renewal. I know that some Christians interpret taking Holy Communion as that, as a sacrament of
renewal, a metaphor of the seasons as well as of the
physical renewal of Christ's body, but just try and get that
experience from your local vicar. He'd ring for the shrink
before you'd swallowed the wine, if he saw that in your
eyes. There is a kind of cruelty I'd want in Christianity,
but it's not their suburban sadism, but what Artaud meant
when he talked about a theatre of cruelty. 'Actors,' he said,
'actors should be like martyrs burned alive, still signalling
to us from their stakes.' Right on, Antonin. That's what's
missing from the theatre, and from the Church, too.
Nothing is sacred. Perhaps it's connected. I don't know.
I'd better not start thinking about it now, or poor old John
through there will be on double overtime. Look, I've
hardly started to say what I want to say about the politics
of sexuality. But do you really want any more?

MS: Keep going.

AR: The lies about passionate love! The hooded winks
wherever you turn! And all of us, even when we're quite
clear-eyed about other subjects, we all go on believing in
the lies, or at least not daring to call out the emperor's got
no clothes on but that's his trip. We all tacitly assent to the
fantasy of a lasting, repeatedly fulfilled, muscle-blowing
union with one partner. It's just the case that we, and as it
happens everyone else we know, has missed out, to date.
And the greatest liar of all would be old Lawrence if he'd
said what we like to think he said, which is a kind of vodka
ad minus the label. Ken Russell filmed it to perfection.
Pour a measure of vodka, add a dash of soft focus, don't
shake or stir anyone, and hup! We like to think that's what
Lawrence said, because what he really said is much more
bitter to swallow than vodka. He required of us – us,
indeed! – that we lay down not merely our modesty, not
our modesty at all in fact, but our ghastly obsession with
our individual personality. Our precious ego, trembling

like a dewdrop on a stalk of grass. Our neurotic need to say, 'this is me, look at me, *I* exist, isn't that amazing, everyone? – and I am this, and this, and I stretch as far as there, but after there it's someone else, oh yes, you can't hold me responsible for what goes on beyond there – but, honestly folks, don't you really, in your hearts, don't you wish you were me? Please? Oh, it's great being me, I can tell you. I'm just sorry you can't be me, too.' And what's ironic is that, in my experience anyway, when two people do make love together beyond the point where their adolescent or commercial fantasies run out, what happens then is precisely what Lawrence told us to hold to, and cherish – we do surrender our personalities, so long as there is generosity in it, warmth, taken into it or generated in the act, it doesn't matter, the result is the same, and a wonder. But afterwards, we start to think, that's not what it's like in the vodka ads. It's not as advertised. It lacked – dramatic shape, somehow. All I did was grind to a halt. It's just not as good, never is, as I thought it was going to be when I was a boy jerking off in the long grass. That's what I've still got to find. Got to. Misery. Then we remember. 'How was it?' 'It was fine,' she says. Like, 'I clicked the shutter just at the right moment. You looked great.'

MS: I'm sorry, I've got to stop you there. John's signalling that we're at the end of the tape.

AR: Can we put another one on?

MS: We could, but to be frank I think we're way off the point of the programme now, terrific stuff though it is.

AR: Look, for my own selfish sake, would you put another one on? Even if I'm wasting the studio time, it's important to me now to finish what I'm saying. I might never get it together again.

MS: Well – have you got another tape handy, John?

[TAPE ENDS]

ANDREW RENGARD: I know what I want to say next.

MARTIN SHY: Right. Fire away then.

AR: At every point of this sick dilemma there are historic and economic reasons to explain it. I'll keep it brief, in deference to your budget. Historically, the concept of romantic love arose in the medieval legends of chivalry. Knights of arms were palely loitering with intent – the belle dame sans merci was in objective fact an accumulation of capital, represented in the dowry, and any wandering knight, dispossessed by the feudal conquests, was badly in need of that. But the desire for money was no theme for a ballad, so it was counterfeited into the desire for an ideal, immaculate woman. I think the truth was exposed by Cervantes, but already it was too late. The new lie people were telling each other about passionate love was that it had to be illicit, adulterous. It was still, in reality, a desire for cash, for the next bourgeois man's property, but now that his actual cash property was not easily to be taken from him, because it was transactions on paper, the new counterfeit excitement was the violation of his wife, who was his property in law and in holy sacrament. All the husbands Don Juan cuckolded were well-to-do bourgeois. What he did was to satirise the equation of property and propriety. It's a comic story, his. But we have lost that laughter now. The fuel that fires our economic engine is a dreary envy. It's fed back to us as the proposition that money and sex are directly exchangeable. One can be cashed in for the other, on demand. Lovely tits will buy you a successful husband. A pile of money brings you status, glamour, power, that you can cash for up-market birds. The earlier periods at least had the shame to cover their lies with metaphor. Not us. We get our cash and spend our seed, and then go out and get more. It's direct from producer to buyer. Male order – that's m,a,l,e, Julia, when you're typing this off. But what if we stopped, and said no, a good orgasm doesn't make me feel one up on the next feller? Doesn't make me feel more singular in the crowd. On the contrary, it makes me more affectionate to the next man, more generous. I am more part of everybody else. If we don't want to be one up, visibly distinct, then why in hell should we buy all the crap we don't need, we just think we want? Wow! Collapse of stout economy. Flash up more bum and tit, quick. You remember how it was when you were innocent, brother? Get it again. Get that big hit you were always looking for when you were a kid in the long grass. You can. You really can. Oh yes. Look at this sheen of thigh – not too closely, brother, not too close, leave her panties on, till you're beautiful and admired and powerful, and then she'll be begging you for it. And it will be like it was always going to be. Promise. They erect a false god only so that they can sell false tributes to it in the market-place. Yet, with the connivance of the Church, as always, they make damned sure nobody, or not many people, are going to go around giving it away. They repress our sexuality and then titillate it, so that our imagination remains as fevered as it was when we were kids. In that fixated fever, shame is bred, not modesty. And not self-recognition, but guilt. Oh, there's no better salesman than guilt for making the cash-registers go ting-a-ling-a-ling. He leaves Abanazar in the shade. Every day he calls out, new lamps for old. See your face, your very own, personalised face, in my shiny lamps. Every day he sells more women their frigidity, guaranteed for years, and men their desperation. All he takes in exchange is a tarnished old generosity of spirit, a trust of body.

MS: Look—

AR: I'm nearly there. Then I'll shut up for good. We don't trust each other's body. We don't trust our own. We are ashamed of it. It is ashamed of itself. Even shame has a price. A man can buy his body liberties with a whore that he would be ashamed to let it perform with his wife. The whore he need never see again. What he is buying is ten minutes of lost identity, ten minutes out of time, his personalised time. It all comes back to our sense of time. Lawrence told us that. He spoke of sexuality as a ritual to plant us again in the universe. Not to exalt our self. Just as Jung distinguished between archetypal dreams and the merely personal ones. If we could surrender our personalised time, so give our self that we forget it, we would not be racked by impatience and anxiety, by envy. We would accept our changes, and each other's. But that would entail an acceptance of death, and how can the personality remain calm before that prospect? We suffer our changes, only, and are impressed by the propaganda of youth. We have expensive watches, and speedometers, and calendars that we throw away on December 31st, except those that, with exquisite aptness, are decorated with lovely naked girls. Those we sell and buy for years afterwards. We are persistently required to write down the date of our birth.

Last paragraph, Julia. Promise. When we talk about revolution, what we are talking about is changing the way we feel for each other. But if revolution liberated us sexually, as a certain kind of revolution would, sex would not be, quote, exciting any more. Sexual fever, the opium of the guilty people, can thrive only when it's sat on by fat toads. But do we dare to kick that junk habit? To ask the question, which came first, property, or sexual fever?

MS: And which goes first?

AR: A voice from the crowd!

MS: Quite. Even if we had time for a tenth of all that, I couldn't use it. It was a remarkable tirade. Do it in a theatre some time. On television it would be ridiculous. I'm not speaking about its content. You can't hector people sitting on their sofas at home, is all.

AR: You can try.

MS: Nice try. But no conversion. As a service to British

32

drama I will ask Julia to type it up and let you have a copy to keep. Do you suppose, if I asked you one last question that I'd like your answer to, you could bring it in inside half an hour?

AR: Ask it.

MS: Why did you get married?

AR: *Why did I get married? I was depressed by the increasing vulgarity of my erotic fantasies. I had run out of imagination.*

MS: That's it?

AR: That's it. That's the kind of thing you want, isn't it?

MS: I want your image of yourself.

AR: I'm not in love with it

MS: All the same.

AR: What will you do with it?

MS: Put it beside Lise's image of you. And the same for her.

AR: A perspective. I see.

MS: Not until I've focussed the images together.

AR: In your own image.

MS: That's right. My image of the images.

AR: It's the next best thing to being God, isn't it?

MS: Yes. No, it's better.

AR: You should know that no one is more offended by blasphemy than the recent apostate.

MS: I can see that. You miss your faith, don't you?

AR: It would take me at least as long to answer that as it did to touch on the politics of sexuality.

MS: I'd be interested. But not until we've switched the tape off.

AR: You're determined that the ideas I hold shall form no part of what you call my image.

MS: It's not that. I hope some trace of them will get into the film, enough for those who are interested to fill in the arguments for themselves. The problem is the banal one of time.

33

AR: The problem of time is not banal.

MS: All right, the banal problem of duration. We quite simply haven't got enough of it to accommodate your arguments. Anyway, even if we had, you'd be wasting your breath. Nothing so offends the British audience as ideas. They wouldn't mind all your talk about sex, if you could only keep it pragmatic.

AR: What Is To Be Done? as Lenin said.

MS: The great pragmatist himself. He also said, reality is slyer than any theory.

AR: I'd like to hear him make out a case for that. The trouble with Lenin is that he's a deviant Marxist. And so is Marx.

MS: Have you lost that faith, too?

AR: That would smack of carelessness.

MS: Isn't Lenin right, don't you think? Don't you come down through theories and systems of ideas to, in the end, living by what you feel on your pulses?

AR: In the end, possibly. I'll let you know, when I get to the end.

MS: At the risk of being offensively crude, isn't it the case that all your theory of sexuality evaporates when you are in bed with Lise?

AR: That is the end, you mean? In any case, the answer is: yes, precisely. That's not the end. That's where it starts from. Starts again, is renewed.

MS: And for Lise, too?

AR: Yes, for Lise, too. Are you getting round to proposing that we be filmed at it?

MS: And then lying back and theorising about it . . . I'd love to, but, unfortunately, while I'm serving out my notice to the company I am still bound by the ethical clauses in my contract.

AR: You're quitting?

MS: Yes. I'll tell you about it. Let's go and have a drink.

[TAPE ENDS]

34

MARTIN SHY: You've talked a little about starting to be an actor. Would you like to talk now about starting to be married?

LISE deWITT: I'll try. What kind of thing exactly do you want?

MS: Start by describing Andrew as you see him.

L deW: Is it all right if I smoke in here?

MS: Sure.

L deW: Andrew is a very – a very complete person.

MS: Mature, do you mean?

L deW: I suppose so, yes. I mean, I suppose that's what I mean.

MS: You don't sound sure.

L deW: Well, no, mature isn't really the right word. *He's still going through a lot of changes, in his ideas, and so on.* And I suppose someone you'd call mature has got past that. You know about his childhood, all the piety, and strictness, and how he broke away from all that when he left home?

MS: Yes, he's told me. But what's your impression of that?

L deW: Well, *somehow he's lost his faith in what he was brought up to believe in, yet he's still so certain about things.*

MS: He's convinced, but he's not sure about what – is that what you mean?

L deW: Yes.

[LAUGHTER]

MS: You say it.

L deW: *He's convinced, but he's not sure about what.*

MS: Not about Marx, for instance?

L deW: He can talk Marxist, and think Marxist in a certain mood, but – he admits it himself – it comes out like lines he's learned. Yet he expresses his opinions as though he had no doubts, even when they are different opinions from the ones he was expressing a year ago. He's

35

even certain about what his doubts are. It's just strength of personality, I suppose.

MS: Is that comforting to live with? Or difficult?

L dew: Both, really. It is difficult, sometimes. *In quite little things it can be difficult. For instance, he's a very tidy person, compulsively tidy really, and I'm afraid I'm not. He was going on the other day about the awful messiness of my dressing-table, which is in our bedroom. He was saying he loved it, all the mess, all the jars with no caps on, and old Kleenex, you know. He wasn't being sarcastic. He never is. He really did, somehow, enjoy the messiness of it all, although he'd tidy up a mess like that anywhere else. And it made me feel disgusted with myself: not at my messiness, because I know I'm messy, but it was as though it was visible proof of the messiness inside me, and he could see right into me.* Because it's my personal stuff, you know, on the dressing-table.

MS: So it was all your ideas with no caps on.

L dew: Exactly. A terrible kind of emotional mess, that I don't seem to have time to tidy up, ever.

MS: And all Andrew's ideas have caps firmly screwed on.

L dew: Yes.

MS: Only he changes the labels from time to time.

L dew: Yes. All this is going to sound like talking behind his back, though, isn't it? It's nice to be able to get things off my chest to you, but that's not the point of what we're doing, is it?

MS: Lise, I've told you, all this will be edited later, and I'll cut out anything you don't want to go into the film.

L dew: But won't Andrew see the transcripts of what we're both saying to you?

MS: Only of what he's said himself. You don't want me to treat you as a couple wholly welded together, do you? As long as you don't leave your transcript on the dressing-table, there's no reason why he should see it.

L dew: No, all right, but – oh, I feel bad about it now, sitting here chatting to you about Andrew and me. The thing is, we do get on fantastically well together. I hope that's going to come across.

MS: I can see you do. But remember we are talking about starting in marriage. There are always difficulties in adjusting to living with someone else. You don't want it to come out twee, do you?

L dew: No, I don't. But please can we switch the tape off for a minute?

MS: If you like.

[TAPE INTERRUPTED]

MS: Right. We're turning again.

L dew: Haven't you got enough yet?

MS: Probably. But I'd like to try and get a bit more.

L dew: All right.

MS: You're sure? If you're still feeling upset, we could leave it for today.

L dew: Oh no, let's try and get it over with.

MS: Andrew said that his relationship with you had, for him, an extra charge in it, from the difference in the class backgrounds you come from. I wonder if you feel the same thing?

L dew: I don't know. Yes, perhaps. I suppose what he's thinking of is all the—This is really awful. We just sit here and discuss what Andrew said, and what he thinks. I feel as though I'm just Mrs Andrew Rengard.

MS: No, what I'm asking you to talk about is your own self, which includes what image of Andrew you have.

L dew: Okay. Look, I'll tell you about the moment when I knew I was in love with him. Big orchestral number behind that line, please. *My parents have got a cottage down in Dorset*, right next to where – this is a joke of Andrew's, need I say? – to where television producers like yourself used to queue up outside Kenneth Allsopp's house in V-formation. *He and I drove down there in my car, just for the day, soon after we'd started going out together. My parents weren't there. It was October, I think. We had a lovely day together, walking on Eggardon Hill, and in the evening we cooked a meal, and then, when it was time to drive back up here, we could hardly see the car from the door of the house. A fog had come down quite suddenly. And I panicked.* I suppose I ought to mention that I was still a virgin then, and the thought of spending the night in the same house on our own was something I wasn't ready to cope with. I rang my mother, and asked her what I ought to do. She said, if we drove very slowly up the lanes we'd probably find that it was just a sea-mist – the cottage is only two miles from the coast – and it would be clear after that. I told Andrew what she had said, and he thought we'd be crazy to try driving through it. Anyway, we did try, and I ran into a wall. It wasn't serious, I'd only scraped a wing, but I was too scared to go on. So somehow we managed to turn the car round and find our way back to the cottage. We'd only gone about half a mile. I simply didn't know what I was going to do when we got there, and it was time to go to bed. *I had this image of Andrew as a kind of young D. H. Lawrence figure, all dark, and working-class, and burning with sexual pride. It was a great image, of course, except now that it had come to the crunch. I was too scared even to speak.* I remember thinking that I'd tell him it was the wrong time of the month, but I didn't expect that to stop him. *And he was marvellous. He understood exactly how I was feeling, and came out completely in the open about it.* He said he thought he was in love with me – he'd never said that before – and that he very much wanted to make love to me, but it would be fatal to our relationship if we did it then, because he could see I was so strung-up, so he was going to sleep in another room, and didn't expect to get a wink of sleep, but it was the best thing. And of course what happened was that I didn't get a wink of sleep myself. And as soon as it was light, in the morning, I brushed my hair, and did my eyes a bit, and made some coffee, and took it into him. He was sleeping like a log! I woke him up with the coffee, and we had a big joke about his sleeping so fast, and in the end I got into bed with him, and that was that. Hey, we can't use that last bit, my mother would flip if she heard me saying that on television.

MS: How soon after that was it that you decided to get married?

L dew: I decided there and then. It took Andrew a bit longer. I knew he was the one I wanted, and I didn't want any nonsense of living in sin with him, partly I suppose because it would have upset my parents, but also because that kind of relationship can easily grow into a habit, and *I felt a proper, deep relationship with Andrew could open up a lot of things for me in acting, a lot of new experience.* I mean, it wasn't for that that I decided to get married, but because I was in love with him; but, given that, then I thought we shouldn't mess about with each other, but really make a commitment, both of us.

MS: Has it helped your acting, would you say?

L dew: I think it's too soon to answer that. It was only in February we got married.

MS: But it's not too soon to ask the question, is it?

L dew: Perhaps not. You're uncannily good at asking me the questions I ask myself. I wish you could answer them, too.

MS: Living with someone from so different a background must have had some effect on you.

L dew: It's certainly made me more aware of my own background, if that's what you mean.

MS: Yes.

L dew: Andrew is so severe. No one had ever treated me severely before. That was a challenge, and I love

39

challenges. I was surprised, though. The conventional picture you get of the working class is a kind of happy-go-lucky, friendly atmosphere, very neighbourly. But Andrew said I'd been taken in by class propaganda, and if I'd ever seen my father giving a working-class man a lecture in court I'd have realised that severity was a normal attitude between the classes, on both sides.

MS: Including his own severity to you?

L dew: Yes, though of course it's different when you're married. And it's not just a class-confrontation thing, severity. His own background was a pretty severe one, though he says he knows other people at home who were like that, too. But it's just an example of what we were talking about, how I've been made more aware of where I've come from. I've realised how un-severe my own family life was, and my friends.

MS: Being more aware of where you've come from is part of knowing who you are, perhaps?

L dew: Absolutely. I'm still finding that out. I suppose – I was thinking, after the last recording we did in here, that maybe the real answer to your question 'Why act?' is just that, to find out who you are. *You try on different parts, and for every one you have to find a new range of gestures, a voice, and so on, and every time it gives you another chance of finding, or building up, a pattern of behaviour which integrates the parts of your own real self. And I wonder whether every actor doesn't have the fantasy that somewhere there is the part which fits his own pattern completely, and he hopes that he might haphazardly find himself playing it one day.*

MS: I wonder about all that. The parts are written for you by somebody else, after all. It's all given.

L dew: No, it's not. You're given the words you say, that's all, but you've still got to ask yourself why this character says this, and how she says it, and what she really means. Who she is, in fact. And then you can go out in

40

front of the audience and feel confident that what you're saying has a real meaning for that character.

MS: And how does that then relate to your own real life?

L dew: Well, you've learned something about someone, and either you recognise a part of yourself in her, or you recognise that you are quite different from her, which is just as relevant.

MS: But this someone that you've learned about isn't real, she's been made up by the playwright.

L dew: Well, all right, but she comes out of some reality of his. And you work at what he gives you to find the reality in her.

MS: My trouble is that I hate the theatre.

L dew: Do you really?

MS: I don't hate actors. It's that self-regarding world of the theatre I can't stand. Whenever I'm dragged against my will into a theatre I watch them up there on the stage compensating for the lack of any drama in their own real lives. Just showing off.

L dew: So it is the actors you hate?

MS: No. It doesn't happen in films, you see. That is because a film is a much purer act of imagination by one man, the director.

L dew: Is this film we're making going to be a pure act of your imagination?

MS: In the end, it has to be. But I'm talking about the cinema.

L dew: You're going to make a cinema film soon, aren't you? Andrew told me.

MS: Yes, when we've done this series, I'm leaving. We've got off the point, haven't we? I think perhaps we should wrap it up for now, but would you mind coming in for just one more session in here? Could you make it on Tuesday next week?

L dew: If you imagine I'm still likely to come up with anything you can use.

41

MS: Don't worry about that.

[TAPE ENDS]

MARTIN SHY: What we were talking about last time was whether your decision to get married, while you're still preparing for a career – a career, incidentally, in which marriage is difficult – was a way of assuring yourself of an identity, beyond the experiments with identity that are the life of an actor.

LISE deWITT: I don't remember any of that.

MS: Perhaps you didn't put it quite like that.

L dew: I may have said something like it. It worries me that, whenever I think back about these sessions in here, I only get a blurred memory of what I've been saying.

MS: Don't worry. You'll see the transcripts later.

L dew: It's not that which worries me. Just that I'm being trained at the school to observe people, and my own response to them, yet I can't get that sort of awareness in this situation.

MS: Have you discussed it with Andrew?

L dew: No. I think that what it is is that it's the first time in my life I've ever been invited to talk away about myself without anyone who's going to contradict me. It's quite an unusual situation.

MS: I have contradicted you, you know. Or at least questioned some of the things you say.

L dew: Yes, I suppose you have.

MS: But you've forgotten.

L dew: Like people forget your face, you say. It's that negative capability again. Your talent for drawing things out of people. It's as though they can make of your face whatever expression they need to see facing them.

MS: I'd love to talk about my face some other time. What about this question of identity? You've talked about Andrew as a severe person. Do you feel his severity as a threat

42

to your identity, or as a challenge that will strengthen it?

L dew: It will stretch me, I hope.

MS: But stretching can snap.

L dew: I won't snap. I'm not the type. I know when the strain is getting too much, and I pull back.

MS: Give me an example.

L dew: I don't think I can. It's internal.

MS: Try to remember something.

L dew: Well. All right, there have been times when Andrew has gone on about my family, the upper-class background and all that, and naturally I resent it, beyond a certain point. I'm not simply and totally the product of my family. There is a me, as well as an it, and it's the me he married. And that me can look back at my upbringing quite objectively, and see it for what it was. And what it was may have been privileged, of course it was, damned privileged, but am I to go through the rest of my life pouring scorn on the people who love me, and whom I love? Or keeping quiet while someone else pours scorn on them? The privilege was only one factor. There was an awful lot else, love, encouragement, fun, sympathy, which have got nothing at all to do with class, or privilege, or anything like that. And the trouble with Andrew is that those are the things he didn't have. It's those things which really matter. And because he lost his mother, and his father is the kind of man he is, a good man, but puritanical, not warm, Andrew didn't get all those things, and, quite naturally, he feels some, I don't know, resentment, I suppose. You can't use any of this. I won't let you. Switch the tape off, please.

[TAPE INTERRUPTED]

MS: That's very good. Say it again, if you can. We've got the tape running again now.

L dew: What, all of it?

MS: No, just the last bit, about rehearsing in a family.

L dew: In a family, you rehearse without any fear of real penalties. But when does real life start? No, I said something else before that.

MS: But when does rehearsing stop. Try it again.

L dew: *In a family, you rehearse without fear of any real penalties. But when does rehearsing stop, and real life start? If you're not part of the reality, you must be part of the illusion.*

MS: That's very good.

L dew: I'm glad I've given you one bit of tape that's not wasted, at any rate.

MS: Just one last question. All right?

L dew: Yes, I'm okay now.

MS: I think people are bound to be interested in how your parents and Andrew's father get on. Can you say anything about that?

L dew: Not much. They only met each other once, at the wedding, and then it was a special occasion, you know, and everyone just said the proper jolly things. I don't think my father would find it difficult to get on with Andrew's.

MS: And your mother?

L dew: Oh, I expect she'd be all right. Only she might find him rather sober. She likes to get everyone thumping their tails – that's one of her phrases – and somehow I can't see Andrew's father's tail thumping much.

[TAPE ENDS]

NOTES ON TREATMENT

Counterpoint two Starting themes – starting in careers (the series theme), starting in marriage (special complication in this film). Which is more difficult? Which matters more to Lise? To Andrew?

Starting in careers: See them going to theatre, to watch

44

professionals. Intercut with them learning the profession at the drama school. Contrast upper-middle class (Lise) and working-class (Andrew) strains in British acting – juxtapose posters on wall of their flat, perhaps Gielgud/Caine, or Richardson/Williamson, or even Sarah Bernhardt/Monroe. Mention insecurity of profession. Quote Mailer on actor's search for identity (in MM book). What is it drives them (and hundreds of other recruits every year)? Vanity? (Fantasy sequence of their names up in lights?) Love of theatre? (See them looking through old programmes of shows they've been to?) Glamour? (Possible sequence in showbiz restaurant, with signed photos on walls, etc.) Need to risk self-exposure? (Fix sequence with masks at drama school – not too heavy, though.) Need to act out the emotions which real life never allows us pure? (Intercut each playing big part with relatively humdrum footage of their everyday lives?)

Starting in marriage: Domestic scenes, contrasted with continuation of what they were when not yet married – ?visit to each of their homes. Working separately and together at drama school. Contrast again of upper-middle/working-class backgrounds. Juxtapose e.g. silver coffee pot (Lise's) with posters of Che, Ho Chi Minh, etc. in their flat. Film Lise driving them (car is hers) to her parents' weekend cottage in Dorset. Hint at problem of sexual adjustment in marriage, any marriage – ?possibly use some of Andrew's spiel on sexuality on W/T over film of e.g. Lise doing her make-up at dressing-table. In visual characterisation, contrast Lise's grace and beauty with Andrew's deftness and tidiness. ?Hint of conflict there – Lise confined by his order, like a swan in a suitcase. That a possible way of explaining, tacitly, chief problem of W/T tapes, Lise's reluctance to speak more than answers to questions, Andrew's self-protecting rhetoric. She is full of supposings, he is full of certainties. Get Manny to see if he can edit down a sequence illustrating that – a tentative thought from Lise, followed by an assertion (on similar subject) from Andrew, repeated several times. Could point up contrast with discreet music track.

Two more points.

1. Should contrast basically conventional choices they have made as Starters with hint at alternatives they have rejected – e.g. in acting, street theatre groups, etc.; in marriage, commune (there is one in City Lane where we might be able to take them on a visit – possibly presented as evening stroll around districts they aren't familiar with, gathering 'colour' for their acting).

2. Perhaps get one of them to read following stanzas by W. H. Auden, re their motives for acting—

> So I wish you first a
> Sense of theatre; only
> Those who love illusion
>   And know it will go far;
>
> Otherwise we spend our
> Lives in a confusion
> Of what we say and do with
>   Who we really are.

(*Many Happy Returns*)

M.S.

Andrew's face had not lost its Celtic sternness for a moment while he was reading the dossier. But now, as he shut the file, he shut his eyes, too, and the line of his lips hardened, toward bitter smiling. If you could see me, he thought, you might interpret this expression as the smile of one who knows just what he is going to do about it all.

46

But I don't. I don't know what I am going to do, now that I have grown up.

As we are already inside Andrew's head, it will be a convenient point of view from which to narrate the story of what happened after Martin Shy had recorded the tapes with him and Lise.

The filming took nearly three weeks. The first week was intensive. Martin, his crew of four, and Julia the PA, would arrive at the flat before Andrew and Lise had finished their breakfast, to start setting up lights and try camera angles. A designer was usually with them, fixing up posters he had bought, photographs and theatre programmes, and arranging the furniture to accommodate the angles Martin wanted. The flat was roomy enough for two people to live in, but when eight or nine were in it, with their equipment, their boxes, lights, tripods and cables, they were crammed in Victorian corners to keep out of shot. One track, following Lise from the bedroom to the kitchen, could not be managed until a carpenter had been brought in to re-hang the kitchen door so that it opened inwards. It became a catch-phrase, whenever Martin said, 'We've got a problem here,' to answer, 'So we re-hang the door.'

The crew, preferring this assignment to the urgency and discomforts of the news stories they more often worked on, were in a cheerful mood. Andrew enjoyed the first week of the work; he liked to be part of a professional team, learning quickly about the techniques of performing for a camera. As for Lise, she couldn't have been tickled more pink.

'You're succumbing to the glamour of telly,' Andrew teased her.

'No I'm not. It's just that it's marvellous to be doing something for a real audience, at last. Anyway, so are you. Look at you, all this week. You've even woken up in a good mood, every day.'

'Yes, but it's not unmitigated cherries. I'm getting just a bit spooked by the way Martin rearranges reality if it's unreasonable enough to defy his camera-angles. Our reality.'

'You mean that Che poster?'

'I mean that Che poster, and that Ho Chi Minh poster, and that book of Sarah Bernhardt pictures—'

'That is reality now. He made a present of it to me.'

'Maybe he's giving me the Che. I'll deface it if he does. Romantic matinee-revolutionary.'

'Why don't you tell Martin it spooks you?'

'I did. He quoted a French poet at me, of whom I had to confess I'd read little. "I hate commonplace things so much that the truth I find boring." Which was so nice that I had to drop the subject.'

'Your trouble is, you can resist everything except quotation.'

'True. Wounding, but true. All the same – you know he's got lines he wants us to say? Lines he's written himself.'

'Yes, I know.'

'Don't you mind?'

'Not if they're good lines. I didn't manage to say many good things of my own in the taping sessions.'

'Well, I'm immodest enough to think I said plenty, and I can't see why I have to be fed lines now.'

The reason, Martin explained when Andrew brought it up again, was that, since objective truth does not exist, to seek it is merely an exercise, a pastime, a stinking sock trailed to assuage the hounds, a chimera, or just imaginably a Medusa, who has struck dumb those few who have gazed upon her, and, Martin said, he was no Perseus, especially when his only weapon was two-dimensional film shot through one lens. The simile, Martin allowed, signalling the wine-waiter to bring them another bottle of burgundy, was not the most inept, because, like Perseus, he too did not look at his quarry, the subject, at the moment of attack, but had to trust the cameraman to reflect it faithfully. 'To that extent, I am never completely in control. When I see the rushes, I'm always surprised.'

'In spite of those waves of metaphor,' Andrew answered, 'I am still at sea. My question was not so much about the film you shoot, but about the words of ours that will be heard. We will be held responsible for them, to a degree that we shan't be for what the viewer actually sees. Why do you find it necessary to give us lines to speak, when you have already recorded so much of both of us?' Andrew looked to Lise for support, but she was watching her glass being filled, not him, so he went on, 'Incidentally, I disagree with you about the non-existence of objective truth, but no doubt that is a character flaw that I owe to a Christian upbringing.'

Martin, who had meanwhile been severe with the partridge on his plate, said, 'I use metaphors deliberately whenever this subject comes up, because all art is metaphor. What is a metaphor? A change transacted through a word, or, literally, a carrying-over of meaning. It is a transformation, a rendering of one thing in the form of another. So form is at the centre of art, and the end of it, too. What you gave me on the tapes we recorded was meaning, crude, untreated. What I am giving back to you is form.'

'But a different meaning,' Andrew answered.

'No.' Martin stabbed a sprout. 'The same meaning, in my metaphor.'

'But it's not our words you're using, when you give us lines. And our meaning is in our words, not yours.'

'Look,' Martin said, 'I can't use all the words we recorded. You know that. Therefore, I have to choose to keep some of them, and to discard others. Already, then, I

49

am rendering your meaning down, into a form chosen by me. Then I add pictures, I may add music, or effects. Also, I re-order the sequence of your meaning, because of course the tapes weren't recorded in any very ordered pattern. By the time I have made so many transformations of what you said to me in the studio, the addition of a few extra lines that you didn't quite in fact say is a marginal brushstroke. Don't you agree with me, Lise?'

Lise had been looking at the autographed photos of actors on the wall beside their table, while chewing a partridge leg held in her fingers. 'Hmmm? Sorry,' she contributed.

Martin went on, 'All this I do, I must do, in order to tell the audience the truth. My truth. As I am sure you will remember, Brecht remarked that you can't just write the truth, you have to write it for, and to, somebody, somebody who can do something with it. How easy my job would be if the truth just existed, like diamonds lying in Kimberley gravel, and the only work required was to pick it up and prize it, and show it off. It has to be wrought. It doesn't exist till then.'

'What you're saying,' Andrew replied, 'is that you're the artist, and we're the sitters.'

'That's how it must be in any film. As opposed to a play, which is communally created, I understand.'

'But this is supposed to be a *documentary* film.'

'That's a label stuck on by the viewers. It has no meaning to the film-maker.'

Andrew rolled his eyes to the ceiling, and in his Gielgud voice said, ' "And would not stay for an answer." '

'Yes, I have a lot of time for jesting Pilate,' Martin replied.

'What are you washing your hands of?'

'Only partridge grease, I'm afraid.' Martin swallowed some wine, and pursed his lips. 'Crucifixion, it must be said, is the very stuff of show business.'

'I've warned you against making blasphemous jokes to me.'

'But you did drop that one in my lap,' Martin said. 'By the way, you dropped a roast potato in your own some time ago.'

'Not on camera, I hope.'

'No, they'd finished shooting.'

'Aren't they coming to eat with us?'

'I'm afraid I can't make the budget stretch that far.'

'So it's cheese sandwiches for the workers, in the caff round the corner.'

'Now you're the one who's jesting. What they get paid on overtime like tonight would be about a week of Equity basic.'

'They could buy themselves a meal here, then.'

'They could, but they wouldn't. They prefer a good simple steak, when they get home to their wives. How's that hare?'

'Oh, very jugged, thankyou.'

'The partridge was delicious,' Lise said, 'don't you think?'

'Yes, it was,' Martin agreed. 'Welcome back.'

'Sorry,' Lise smiled. 'You did tell me to look at the photos, though.'

'When they were filming. They finished twenty minutes ago.'

'I know. But it's just extraordinary how everyone you can think of in the theatre is stuck up here, somewhere, if you look long enough.'

'What they remind me of,' Andrew told Martin, 'is all those butterflies in glass cases you've got stuck up around your house. So beautiful, and so dead.'

'Why dead?' Lise asked. 'They're not dead yet, most of these people.'

'Oh yes they are,' Andrew answered, 'shot with a camera. Anyway, half of them were never alive, if you saw them on stage. Being photographed, and then signing it, was what they were best at.'

'You are incredibly arrogant about the theatre,' Martin said. 'Really. What I've been saying about my profession is the sweetest modesty in comparison.'

'Do they serve humble pie here?' Andrew asked.

'Those people,' Martin went on, 'are like my butterflies, though not in the sense you meant. Their beauty is a function of survival in the environment they inhabit. Perhaps they are somewhat self-regarding. Perhaps a butterfly is, too. Why not? It's survived. It's come through the fine, cruel sieve of evolution. That is a justification for occasionally glancing at your wings over a pond. And those people have somehow struggled and survived in what you know well is a torment of a profession, yet you can just dismiss the lot of them with—'

'Not the lot of them,' Andrew interrupted. 'Half of them was my modest estimate.'

'Oh, Andrew,' Lise said, prettily pouting with impatience. 'Martin's right. He banged the nail right on the head. It's marvellous to hear someone who's not an actor pay a tribute like that to the profession. And all you do is keep up this pose of—'

'Pose? Something I've said to you virtually every day since we met, a pose?'

'Yes, it is a pose, all the same. You envy them, really, just as I do, only I don't feel the need to dress up my envy in some verbose theory about the workers' theatre, or whatever it is.'

'Lise,' Andrew said, quietly now, 'come on, you know me better than that.'

'I know you well enough to know what's posing and what's real in you.'

'Do you? Truly?'

Then Lise started to cry.

'You know I hate it when you cry,' Andrew said to her, the next morning. 'That's why I walked out, not because of the argument. I was enjoying that.'

'I wasn't,' Lise answered, deftly defining the line of her eyelid in the mirror. 'You should have seen that.'

'Well, I didn't. I thought you weren't taking much notice of him or me, just letting us get on with it. I was surprised when you started to cry. I didn't—'

'All right, let's forget it now. Perhaps I was a bit tired, with all this filming and the script to learn.'

'You don't need to learn those lines he's given you. You can fix them in your head just before they shoot it.'

'I mean the Isabella lines he wants me to do. Anyway, I don't agree about the other lines. I can't just do them cold. If they are to sound as though it's me speaking, I need to rehearse them first.'

'You realise what you're doing? – rehearsing the part of yourself, that he has written for you. How phoney can you get?'

'No, I think Martin's right. We talked about it last night, after you'd walked out.'

'What did he say?'

'Pretty much what he'd said to you, about art being a necessary lie to get at the truth. So we re-hang the door.'

'That took three hours?'

'No, we talked about a lot of other things, too. It helps me, talking to him. He's very understanding.'

'Thanks very much.'

'Don't be a silly.'

'Did you stay in the restaurant all that time?'

'No, we walked by the river for quite a while, after we'd finished the meal. You made a big mistake, leaving before the profiteroles.'

'While I was sitting here, wondering where the hell you'd got to.'

'It was your fault for just walking away.'

53

'You could have rung.'

'To say what?'

'Where you were.'

' "Andrew, darling, I'm walking by the river with Martin." Would that have made it better for you?'

'Yes.'

'All right, next time I will.'

'Is that a threat?'

'Do you mind if I talk to another man sometimes?'

'To him I do, yes.'

'Oh God, you are frightful in the mornings.'

'I'll still be fraightful about this at midnight.'

'Andrew, you've really no cause to be like this. What is wrong if someone else happens to understand some things that are on my mind, and it does me so much good to talk to him about them?'

'I want to be everyman to you.'

'If I said that to you, you'd call it sexual imperialism.'

'Right. It's also called love.'

Martin had arranged with the Principal of the drama school that Andrew and Lise should be filmed there rehearsing a scene between Angelo and Isabella in *Measure for Measure*, the scene in which Angelo asks her to sleep with him. The end-of-term production was, in fact, to be *Romeo and Juliet*, with Andrew and Lise in the title parts, and the researcher, recommending them to Martin as subjects for his film, had called that a 'big plus filmwise'. Martin disagreed: it would be corny television. Privately, he told Andrew he was surprised that the Principal should be so sentimental in his casting. The Principal, anyway, raised no objection to what Martin wanted to stage. Watching a television crew at work with actors would be a valuable experience for his students, he said. Andrew knew that it would be a valuable experience in professional envy for every one of them. So what? Should he urge them to let it all hang out, in some epic session of Maoist self-criticism? Just that is what he might have done a month earlier, before this television game began. 'Experience unteaches,' he would have remarked. Now he had other problems, of his own.

There was the taped passage in which he had told the story about meeting his old headmaster, and not telling the man what he truly thought of him for fear of embarrassing his father's position in the small-town community. Martin had pointed out the spotlit paradox that saying it on television would be several million times more embarrassing. Yes, Andrew agreed, he had said it to Martin only because it was too easy, in that intimate, proofed studio to forget that the world was eavesdropping. Nevertheless, to cut that bit of tape now would compound the shame he felt at not having told the headmaster how he felt. He wanted to keep it in, because if he really believed in the necessity of changing society (as he had said he did elsewhere on the tapes) then he would be crass to let slip this opportunity, that Martin had presented to him, of speaking the truth through the most powerful loudspeaker that society offered. The embarrassment to his father was a sacrifice that Andrew was prepared to make, remorsefully, in order to exploit the greater good of social action. But, Andrew asked, it would be less embarrassing to his father, would it not, if Martin cut the part where Andrew had said, precisely, that he was nervous of embarrassing him? Martin's view, however, was that the story had no meaning, in the personal context of the film, without Andrew's remarks upon his own feelings. It could all stay in (provisionally – one never knew how it was going to look a week longer into the editing), or all hit the bin, but no half measures. What did Manny think?

Manny, the film editor, wanted to keep it all in. 'That

way, with the story and your comments on yourself, the whole sequence is self-cancelling.'

'And that's a good thing?' Andrew asked.

'Yes. Otherwise you leave people with the idea that progress can be made.'

'And it can't be?' Andrew asked. But Manny just shook his head, his small, bespectacled, grey head, that never liked to talk for long, except when it was very drunk, at a party, and then Manny would purify his accumulated rancour by declaiming passages of *Das Kapital* from memory, stripping the clothes from himself in the heat of his frenzy. When Andrew heard about such performances, from Martin, he asked Manny if he was a Marxist.

'I was once,' Manny replied, 'but I found it too optimistic.'

Andrew was preoccupied also with the problems of filming with Martin. It was not only the invented lines that Lise and he were required to say: Lise apparently had no objection to hers, and Andrew, for his part, had reached agreement with Martin that he could re-phrase the given lines in words more authentically his own. Thus, Martin's 'I don't feel confident about the world into which our baby will be born' became 'What a world to give a child to. What a world to give a child.' Martin conceded that Andrew's version was crisper, though later he cut it altogether, because it sounded, indeed, like a line, too prepared. It was Martin's delight, when filming, in the accidental that worried Andrew, more than the invented lines and staged angles did.

At the end of the second week of shooting, for example – by now they were spending more time at the studios, watching rushes, and editing, than they were out with the crew – Martin took them to be filmed watching a street theatre group at work. The group were paid a facility fee for their appearance in the film, and were amenable to doing several takes for the camera. Their

56

show was a political one, in support of the workers at a local bread factory, who were on strike in protest at the sacking of two of their colleagues. In the scene Martin had arranged to film, two of the Workers stuffed the Boss's mouth full of sliced bread, then spread margarine and raspberry jam on top, all over his face. On the first two takes, the sound engineer had a hitch. On the third, the Boss, his throat by now desiccated, threw up. Martin signalled to the cameraman to keep it turning. On the rushes, Andrew and Lise saw that the focus had been pulled, first to include their faces, then to close in on them, wearing expressions of appalled comedy.

'But if you use that take,' Andrew said, 'the viewers will have no way of knowing that that man throwing up is not part of the normal show they do. Nor of knowing that our response was to the accident, not to the group's work.'

'It works,' was all Martin would say. 'It works,' or 'It just doesn't work, that's all,' was, by now, all he would say about most of the rushes they watched. And Andrew, in frustration, felt unable to argue him dialectically further, because, in his own profession, he knew how inexplicable the alchemy of art is, how a performance, analysed and anatomised, will reserve some atomic core, infinitely compressed, that cannot be probed, or even described, yet which irradiates the work, and those who see it.

'Explain it, and you explain it away,' he admitted, late one night, drinking Scotch and water at Martin's house, among the boxes of pinned butterflies, where Mrs Shy had cooked them a fine, five-course meal. 'Come over to my place tomorrow evening, and we'll split a bottle, and a few hairs,' Martin had invited them the previous day, on the way back from Dorset, where they had been filming at Lise's parents' cottage. Andrew was glad to accept, hoping to speak alone with Martin about Lise. He was troubled by a moodiness in her that he had not known before.

'It's her pregnancy,' Martin said, taking hold of

Andrew's ankle outstretched from an armchair. 'I've seen it in Sybil, every time. The spirit turns inward, toward the womb. While they are going through the motions of their normal lives, with you and me and everyone else, it's as though we were distracting them from the focus of their bodily attention. Sometimes they're just as we have always known them, and then a shutter will snap down, and they are seeing not just through you but clean to both ends of eternity.'

'That's it,' Andrew agreed. 'I recognise all you've just said.'

'I envy it,' Martin remarked. 'I envy any bodily experience I can't have myself. There aren't many.'

'And the birth, do you envy them that?'

'Yes, that too, that most of all, I suppose, despite the pain of it.'

'Were you there when your kids were born?'

'What did you do in the Great Birth, Daddy? No. I stink of cowardice when someone else is in pain.'

'I want to be there.'

'The God you once believed in didn't, in my opinion, make as wonderful a job of the human body as the sentimentalists like to say. I mean, for instance, to cobble an excretory channel into the sexual organ, what a cheap, gimcrack job. Any plumber would do better. The trouble it has caused, over the years.'

Andrew was too full of Martin's food to reproach him.

'I believe,' Martin went on, 'that on the eighth day He had that Monday morning feeling, and He's never shaken it off. He should have declared a perpetual St Monday.'

Sybil and Lise had come in with some coffee for them. 'Martin's going on about God again,' Andrew told them. 'I'm past caring.'

'That's a good thing,' Sybil said, 'because Martin never gets tired of it. He thinks God's got it in for him.'

'I'm amazed,' Andrew answered. 'It didn't occur to me

that you took God seriously enough to believe anything at all about Him.'

'Oh, I don't believe in Him,' Martin said. 'But I'm convinced He believes in me.'

Sybil, blonde, half-Czech, older in appearance than her husband, was proud of him, her children, and her Georgian house. When one of them let her down, there were always the others. Andrew and Lise never heard her speak of anything else. She contrived to make them feel fortunate indeed to be filmed by her husband. He, of course, was 'going into movies' soon. That was where Martin was at. There, and at anyone's mercy, were it not for her, behind him, like a shadow, shadowing him.

Perhaps, Andrew thought, I should be reassured by her. With a wife like that, he cannot be more than a gay dog in the manger. If, then, all that attracts Lise to him is that 'understanding' she attributes to him, jealousy in me is paltry. I should be man enough to be glad that she has someone to guide her through the marshlands of her growing mind that I, myself, happen to know nothing about. She will, in the end, come back to terrain where I have had the experience to help her. It is her pregnancy, Martin says, that takes her away from me at present; and, as the father of three children, he knows that journey well. Of all the problems that I have been sorting into suits, this is the least.

Andrew had to direct his smile of relief at someone, and bestowed it upon Sybil, who started uncertainly to smile back at him, then stopped, and looked away crossly, as one who is teased. Perhaps she had read it as a fresh smile: so Andrew said, 'That was a marvellous meal, Sybil. Thank you.' She only flickered her lips irritably in reply, so Andrew went on, 'It has been so enjoyable, this filming with Martin, that to get paid a fee for it seems like taking money on false pretences.'

'What money isn't?' Martin said.

Lise's smile, now, at Martin, was so quick and warm as to siphon off all the relief Andrew had felt. He went back to worrying about the time Martin and Lise had been spending together. When they were all out filming, the two of them talked in corners, ostensibly about what was required of Lise in the next shot. She pretended it was a tribute to Andrew that he needed so much less direction. But, after that first walk by the river, there had been other meetings, other walks, outside the shooting schedule and, no matter the pain in Andrew's dark, Celtic face, Lise was tersely determined, each time, that she had the right to go on talking with Martin.

'It can't all be director's notes?' Andrew had enquired.

'No,' she said, 'I told you, it's more general.'

'What, in general?'

'Things that came out of the tapes I recorded with him.'

'You mean, he's trying to sort some of it into lines you can say on film?'

'No, just – oh, you know, I told him a lot of things about myself, on the tapes, things I didn't even know until I said them, and he seemed to understand so well even though I couldn't explain them properly. It really helped me a lot, with myself, you know? So all we do, when I see him, is carry on from where we'd got to on the tapes.'

'Can you tell me what kind of things you mean? Are they things you've told me about?'

'Not all of them, no.' Lise smiled, not aggressively, at Andrew. 'But there's no great secrets I share with him. A lot of the time we're talking about when I was a kid.'

'Well, we've talked about that a good deal, too.'

'Yes.'

Andrew had left it at that. Another row about it could only stiffen their attitudes. He decided to believe what Lise had said. As for Martin, he once remarked to Andrew, 'On my own, I get lonely. I don't have the inner life that people like you seem to have. I need the outside world all the time.

If that's not exciting, I'd rather go to sleep.' All right, so Lise it was who kept him awake, for now. Andrew did not feel slighted. Lise is a lovely girl, and Martin likes to help her.

After the meal, outside the Shys' house, Martin took Andrew on one side while Lise was opening the car. 'Lise told me she thought you were worried about the talks she and I have been having. Don't worry. She's going through a change. There's nothing you can do about it, meanwhile, except to wait till she comes through it. She will.'

'That's the conclusion I'd reached myself,' Andrew smiled.

'Good. See you tomorrow.'

The next day was the last of filming. The location was a commune, in a tall, narrow old house at the rundown edge of the district where Martin lived. The oriental and macrobiotic decor were so stereotyped that Andrew suspected the whole set-up had been created by the designer, and probably cast by Martin. 'Not at all,' Martin assured him. 'It was dressed as nature intended when the researcher found it. Not that it took much finding. They're cigar-store Indians.'

Lise was talking to a girl suckling a baby. In a very quiet voice, the girl explained that the baby's father did not live in the commune. Andrew looked at Martin's script. It required him and Lise to ad-lib a conversation with someone called Pete about 'nuclear family/extended family', starting with a scripted question for Lise, 'Don't you believe that the need for one father and one mother is biological, not just conventional?' Behind him he heard, in a low tone, the crew's litany of 'Camera running. Mark it. *Bleep*. Synch.' Seeing the sound man crossing the floor like a crab, holding a mike, Andrew realised that Martin had decided to start filming Lise and the girl without

61

warning them. He walked into shot, still holding the script, and motioned with his eyes to alert both girls to the mike. 'I'm surprised,' he said to the suckling girl, 'that you agreed to let the Machine in here.'

She looked up at him, with friendly eyes, a few years older than he'd thought at first, shaking her long hair, not understanding.

'Television,' Andrew said. 'I'd have thought it was one of the monsters you're cutting free from, in a commune.'

'We don't mind,' she answered. 'Everyone is welcome here.'

'But isn't there something incongruous in an alternative society that permits straight society to exploit it for its entertainment?'

'No,' she said, simply.

'We can use the bread,' said a man standing in the doorway, and now joining the group. 'We have to get it somehow, and this is no hassle.'

'I'd have expected you to object on principle,' Andrew said. 'Do you have principles, in the commune?'

'Yes, of course,' the man said.

'Can you say what they are?'

'Sharing. Supporting. Being spontaneous.'

'No rules at all?' Lise asked.

'No rules, only voluntary agreements. We believe in Anarchism. Only the problem with saying that is that people seeing this will assume that we throw bombs at people, because that's how the word "Anarchist" is used. But we're not that sort of Anarchist. When we started, with some other people who've split now, we were into Kropotkin, and that's still our bible, if you like, *Mutual Aid*.'

'The question I'd like to ask you,' Andrew said, 'is – No, the argument I'd like to put to you is that if you believe our society is evil, or anyway sterile, your duty is to take action to change it, for everyone's sake, not just to take a personal trip out of it.'

'Nobody here is on a personal trip,' the man said. 'The commune itself is the trip, if you like.'

'All the same, it's an alternative just for yourselves.'

'Yes, at present.'

'You mean you hope to bring about social change by example?'

'Who knows? If other people like the look of the way we live, and decide to do something about themselves, then that's great.'

'But it's not your purpose?'

'We don't need that sort of purpose. We don't have to justify ourselves to anyone outside the commune. And we don't want to lay our ideas on other people.'

'In other words, you're not concerned about social change?'

'No,' the man said, patiently.

A dark-haired girl who had come in behind the man said, 'When people like you are interested enough in us to want to put it on television, that's some kind of social effect, isn't it?'

Andrew answered, 'I'm not, and Lise's not, people like you mean.'

'You're into television, aren't you?'

'Just for now.'

The girl smiled knowingly.

'Well, so are you, now,' Andrew accused her.

'The difference is,' she said, 'that tomorrow we can live without it again. This is just a bread scene, to us. What we'd call an experience of ecstasy is just the opposite of an ego-trip.'

'I'm on no ego-trip,' Andrew said, breathing from his diaphragm.

'Of course you are. You're actors, aren't you? You are really into that heavy buzz it gives you. We don't need false eyelashes.' The girl was looking at Lise, but spoke without scorn. 'We want to find out what we are, for each other. We got this thing together so as to get *away* from all the bourgeois fictions we had been brought up to believe in, and people told us were necessary, like girls have got to have sex-appeal, and men have to have money.'

'That's right,' the man said. 'What we're doing is finding out what is necessary.'

'But—' Andrew said.

'Cut,' Martin said.

'Can we put another magazine in?' Andrew asked him. 'I want to go on with this.'

'You can go on with it,' Martin told him, 'but I've got enough of it on film already. There's no point in reloading.'

Meanwhile, the dark-haired girl had told the man something, and both had left. The baby, too, had had enough, and was being winded by its mother, watched by Lise. The crew started to pack up.

'Wait a minute,' Andrew said, addressing the whole room. 'We'd hardly begun to get into the argument.' Everyone was preoccupied, and assumed that he was speaking to someone else.

'We've got some mute cut-aways to do,' Martin told Andrew and Lise, 'but we don't need you for them. I'll meet you in the canteen for lunch.'

'Don't I have to do that line about the biological need for one father and mother?' Lise asked.

'You did it when you looked at that baby,' Martin told her. 'We were tight in on you. You did it beautifully.' He took the script from Andrew's hands, and tore it across. 'Didn't she?'

The commune rushes, early the next week, upset Andrew again. 'It was like a duel in the dark, what we said to each other,' he complained to Martin. 'Come the dawn, and I think they'd find they and I were wearing similar uniforms, or at least that we belonged to allied armies. But from what you actually see on the screen the viewers would think we were implacably opposed to each other.'

'It will look different when we've cut it,' Martin reassured him.

'You keep saying that. When do we get to see a rough assembly, and have all these opportunities you've been promising us of cutting out what we don't like?'

'Of discussing anything which worries you,' Martin corrected him. 'The final decision has always got to be mine.'

'So we re-hang the door again,' Andrew said, and walked quickly out of the viewing theatre.

He didn't want to leave the studios without Lise, so he went to see Manny in the cutting room, along the corridor. Manny was working on the restaurant sequence. The frame on the Steenbeck screen was a close-up of Lise sinking her teeth into a melon. She looked like Venus attached to her prey. 'What does it mean?' Andrew asked, still short in temper.

'I don't know,' the editor confessed. 'Martin asked me to build up a montage of several shots of Lise eating. He wants to mix through five or six of them, slowly.'

'Have you got that many? I didn't have much idea of where the camera was pointing.'

'We've got about sixteen, at a guess.'

'And what's on the soundtrack? Gnashing of teeth?'

'I haven't been told, yet. I think he wants just music. He said something about Mozart.'

'Wolfgang Amadeus Mozart?'

'Probably.'

'With that. Can I see it run through?'

'It's not mixed yet, of course.' Manny finished the join he was making, ran pictures of Lise frantically repealing bites into food, then ran it forwards at normal speed. Andrew whistled *Eine Kleine Nachtmusik*. 'I think,' Manny observed, 'he has a piano concerto in mind.'

'Don't tell me – the slow movement of the 24th.'

'Funny you should say that.'

'You mean it.'

'I believe so.'

'What does it mean, Manny?'

'All the great clichés should be tried out, once.'

'But not all at once.'

The sequence ended. 'It's very well lit,' Manny remarked.

'You mean Lise looks gorgeous.'

'Yes, doesn't she.'

'Manny . . .' Andrew looked at him, and shook his head. 'What kind of film is this that I'm in?'

'I don't know,' Manny said, and cackled.

'I must have been crazy to let myself in for it all. I've never even seen any film he's made before. Were they good?'

'One was,' Manny answered. 'Martin Shy has made one good film, he is making this one, therefore Martin Shy is living on this syllogism for the rest of his career.'

'He's riding it into the movies.'

'So I hear.'

'I get the impression you're not fond of him.'

'You'd have to look hard to find anyone in these studios who is fond of anyone else.'

'Not all that hard, not after seeing what Martin has made of Lise.'

Andrew went back to the viewing theatre, but it was empty. In Martin's office, Julia the PA told him that Martin had just taken Lise back to the flat. But the flat was empty, too. Lise came in three hours later, looking happy. She had only been for a drive with Martin, she answered.

'For three hours? How's it looking in Aberdeen?'

'We were parked most of the time, just talking.'

'Lise, my love, if you won't tell me the truth, we are damned souls, the three of us. No, the four of us.' Andrew indicated Lise's belly.

'There is nothing to tell you, Andrew. We just talked, about things. I'm not telling you any lies.'

'About things. As usual.'

'Yes. As usual. Can't you see how much good it's doing me? Do you resent it that another man can help me, and make me happy?'

Andrew's eyes were hot. He shut them, and very slowly said, 'You are my life. If I lost you, it would be like a part of me being torn off. And I am scared of losing you, I admit it.'

'You're wrong to be scared,' Lise said quietly. 'Martin would never leave Sybil and his kids.'

'You have discussed it, then.'

'No, I simply know it's true, from what he's said about them.'

Andrew lifted the white telephone, and dialled Martin's home number. 'Don't,' Lise asked him. He gripped the telephone to his ear and gazed at her. But there was no answer, and by the morning dreams had re-programmed his anger into a thick, grey dejection.

How could Andrew complain to Martin that his film made Lise look very beautiful? Every day, now that the shooting was finished, they were rehearsing *Romeo and Juliet* at the drama school, and every day Andrew fell in love with her again, with the frail, sad, burning sapphire that she was making of the part. Without Shakespeare's assistance, he would have been speechless before her. 'You're playing it for the romance,' he accused her. 'We agreed, remember?, that the vital subtext is how the two rival families are engaged in a primitive capitalist war, and their two most beautiful children are simply economic hostages, investments, prized coins in the transaction. Their deaths are the triumph of the property instinct over the erotic impulse, which threatens to destroy the capitalist nexus in Verona. The way you're doing it, everybody is going to be too busy crying over young lovers to take any notice of the economic relations that really destroy them.'

Lise answered, 'I'm working at this part as I've never worked before. I'm trying out every line, every word, for what I can find in it. I think it will be the first performance I've ever given which is truly mine, not an assembly of memories of what other actors have done with the part. I want to achieve it, for myself. If what you've just said is in the part, then I'll find it there.'

'It's not just a question of your part. You've got to look at the whole play.'

'That's the director's job.'

And the director, Andrew knew, would not deflect Lise from what she was doing. He was an unreconstructed old Romantic, a failed pro director who had joined the school's staff in the bad, postwar years, and was not to be edged out now by any bright young graduate with a head full of neo-Brechtian theories.

Andrew's dreams are being ripped off him like protective skins. He screams, silently, smiling Good-day to acquaintances. Soon he will have no skin. He will be flayed, open to all infections. Poor devil, he has got a bad time coming. If he could look twenty pages ahead, he would resign from the book.

'I don't quit,' he told Martin.

'But if you're that worried about the play, maybe it would be the braver choice.'

'I'd rather stay inside a situation, and do what I can to

68

change it. Quitting *Romeo* would be like dropping out of society, a vertical act, for the ego, making no contribution on the social plane.'

'I don't, myself, know how anyone who calls himself an artist can set out to work on the social plane,' Martin said. 'What we are about to see' – they were sitting on stools in Manny's cutting room, waiting while the rough-cut was laced up – 'will be seen by up to half our society simultaneously, when it goes out. How can I conceivably make a film for twenty million people at once? I can feel sorry for a spastic child, if I meet one, but how could I feel sorry for thousands of damaged children whom I know only by report, or assumption? I'd be a hypocrite.'

'By trusting your imagination to remind the viewer of his own experiences,' Andrew suggested.

'Which viewer do you have in mind? If you try to envisage an audience on the scale of television, it's just a colossal mob, punch-drunk by horrors on the news and sugar cubes in-between. If you put on lions fighting Christians, I doubt if you would arouse a flicker in their jaded bodies, except at the RSPCA. But make a film for just a couple of people in a room, as I kept saying to you weeks ago, and suddenly you're in the business of communicating.'

'Ready?' Manny asked.

Martin nodded. 'Interest me,' he said, to no one in particular. 'That's the only honest direction a director can give you.'

Manny pressed the green button, and the other three leaned forward.

The first shot was a close-up of Lise's beautiful face speaking Auden's verses about 'a sense of theatre'. During the second stanza, the camera pulled back to see that she was sitting on a chair, in the middle of an empty room at the drama school, holding a pair of knitting needles poised, with half a baby's jacket on them.

69

'I didn't know you could knit,' said Andrew, who had not been there when they shot the sequence.

'I can't,' Lise whispered. 'They got the wardrobe to do that much for me.'

By now the film had cut to a shot of Andrew rehearsing a duel. On wildtrack his voice was remarking, 'Why did I get married? I was depressed by the increasing vulgarity of my erotic fantasies. I had run out of imagination.' The shot closed in on his sternly smiling face.

'One of the several things I'd like to say about that bit,' Andrew told Martin, 'is that I'm duelling with Tybalt in *Romeo* there. I thought we were pretending to rehearse *Measure for Measure*?'

'No one will be bothered by that,' Martin assured him. 'If they are, it's just exercises you're doing.'

Cut to a 2-shot in the flat, with Lise's wildtrack voice hoping that marriage would open up new experiences in her acting. Andrew, in synch sound, is seen to straighten a picture, and mention that the windows could do with a clean.

'Very ironic,' Andrew muttered.

'After four takes, it should be, already,' Martin replied.

The domestic sequence continued, mute. 'There's voice over, here,' Martin said, 'explaining about the drama school. We've still got to lay that track, and the music.'

The picture cut to Andrew saying,

Nay, women are frail too.

Lise responded,

Ay, as the glasses where they view themselves;
Which are as easy broke as they make forms.

The synch sound was faded down, to allow Andrew on wildtrack to be heard defining the social implications of theatre, and Lise admitting to an obsession with acting, after which Shakespeare was given another whirl, before the picture cut to Lise as a baby. She grew beautifully up, in a succession of stills (borrowed, at Martin's request, from the deWitt family album), while her voice described a happy childhood, family visits to the theatre, and asked when the rehearsing had to stop and the real living start. 'If you're not part of the reality, you must be part of the illusion.'

'That's very good,' Andrew told her.

'It's the only good thing I do get to say.'

'She's wrong,' Martin interjected. 'You'll see.'

The stills of Andrew from his father's album were fewer, and more formal. The first one, his mother's face, stern like his, above her arms that cradled and held her only child close to her flower-printed frock, staring at the camera with a frowning smile that could have been puzzled or fierce, but would anyway be cremated within the year – a picture he had seen every day for years upon his father's mantelpiece, it shocked him now, its poignancy projected on a screen for anyone to take a look at, be interested. From the late 1940s, the photograph spoke to Andrew of an age far back in living memory. It was not a picture of his own life, but belonged to the epoch of his parents' own childhood, the decade of the Great War: yet in which he, as though in some previous incarnation, had been born and taught to lisp, and to lose the woman who loved him. He heard his own voice talking about its puritanical upbringing, how it had quit university and knocked around until it entered the drama school. He hated the voice, which he could not connect with his own breathing, now. On it went, the voice, while the few stills of his adolescence gave way to film of Lise driving him to Dorset, and leading him into the cottage. Her voice took over, telling of their first visit there, when Andrew had understood her feelings. The camera tightened on Lise's face, while Andrew's voice said that she was beautiful, mixed-up, English, and that it had got a kick

71

from her class. Then the soundtrack stopped, and several mute shots of Lise went through.

'We'll be mixing here,' Martin said.

The montage ended with a jump cut to a grotesque papier-mâché mask of a Boss, surmounting a figure wrapped in waxed paper, like a loaf. It was the street theatre group, but the scene was one that Andrew did not recognise.

'No,' Martin said, 'I got them to do it later for us.'

The picture cut to Andrew and Lise watching the show, and Andrew's voice, that damned voice, went on again about the training of an actor to be an instrument. 'I hate every word I hear myself saying,' Andrew commented.

'So do I,' Lise agreed. 'At least you express a few ideas. I just twitter.'

'You can't possibly judge your own performances objectively, at this stage,' Martin reassured them. "That's what I'm for.'

Meanwhile, the restaurant footage was purring through the machine, with synch chat about the theatrical life, unquote, fading under Lise's wildtrack explanation that by trying on different parts you find out about yourself. That wildtrack overlapped the start of the next film sequence, in which Lise was seen at her dressing-table, with Andrew in the background of the mirror shot. Lise's voice went on to contrast Andrew's tidy-mindedness with her own disorder, and to mention the perverse pleasure he took in the messiness of the dressing-table now exposed. The commune sequence was next: in the course of it, while the dialogue went on, the picture occasionally cut in contrast to Andrew's and Lise's 2-shot existence in their flat.

'It's still not working,' Manny said.

'No, but we're getting closer to it,' the director answered.

The cross-cutting resolved into a long-held shot of the

two of them in the flat, at the end of a tired day. 'The best bit of acting we did,' Andrew said, in reference to the fact that the film had been shot one morning. The camera panned across a silver coffee-pot, Lise smoking a cigarette and reading an illustrated Life of Sarah Bernhardt, Andrew lying on his back staring, if the camera movement did not lie, at posters of well-known actors and guerrilla fighters. On the soundtrack was heard a short version of Andrew's story about meeting his old headmaster, with some reference to his father's gullibility: 'my father belongs to one of the subject tribes in that field.'

The final sequence was one filmed at the drama school, an acting exercise in which a mask was thrown around a circle of actors, and no one could speak except when holding the mask over his face. Lise's voice was heard on wildtrack, saying that Andrew was going through a period of change, having lost his faith. 'He's convinced, but he's not sure about what.'

The tail end chattered on the bobbin. Manny switched it off, and for several seconds no one spoke. Then Andrew said, 'Is that really how you see it ending?'

'Yes,' Martin answered. 'Don't you like it?'

'I loathe it all. But the ending is weird. Lise says I'm going through a change. Maybe I am. But doesn't it need balancing with some comparable remark from me, on her?'

'The same remark, you mean,' Martin said.

'Well, yes.'

'Let the viewers figure that out for themselves. I hate balanced endings. What's called a well-made programme is boring, because it doesn't take the viewer into account. It pretends to have an existence independent of the viewer.'

There was another silence, punctuated by Martin. 'Perfect art is bad art,' he added. Then he turned to Lise. 'What did you think?'

'Oh God,' she groaned. 'It's not your fault. You've got a lot out of it. I just feel I didn't put much into it, of me.'

'I feel the opposite,' Andrew said. 'I put too much in. There's several things I'd like to cut.'

'Like?' Martin asked.

'Well, the commune stuff, of course. And me talking about a trained instrument for acting, over the street theatre group, makes me sound pretty arrogant.'

'We've still got to get about ten minutes out altogether,' Martin said. 'I might do some trimming there. But at this stage I'd rather you relied on my judgment. You're too close to it.'

'But you said we could cut any wildtrack we didn't like at transcript stage,' Andrew reminded him.

'You didn't ask for any particular cuts then, though,'

'There was never a moment when you seemed to be waiting for us to point to exactly what we'd like to see cut. We were always getting on with the next thing.'

Martin shrugged. 'We're recording the voice-over and music tracks on Tuesday, and Manny's got to dub it by the end of the week, I think?' Manny nodded. 'It's too late to think about re-editing the whole thing from the start,' Martin went on. 'I'm sorry if you feel I've reneged on my promise. I don't think I have. But I'm sure you'll feel differently when you see the finished print.'

'I shan't,' Lise said. 'You know what I wish now? I wish I'd never even tried to put anything of myself into it. I should have deliberately created a part I could play better than I can play myself.'

'Don't worry,' Martin said, 'I've done that for you. It's all metaphor, I explained that. In fact, the title I'm going to give it is *Make Up*. Do you like it?'

Manny made a noise like a bark, but whether it was a laugh, or cough, or the latter disguising the former, it was impossible to read on his melancholier-than-thou face, as Martin called it.

* * *

As Martin called it, **Martin called it, Martin**, Martin, Andrew thought, opening his eyes again and blinking at the strip-lighting in Martin's office, where he had read the dossier, still on his lap. In that discussion programme the night the film went out, we should have staged it so that he walked into the studio to shouts of 'Author! Author!' It might at least have saved that poor critic from stumbling around in the marsh mist where the borders of documentary and fiction are no better than the surmises of early cartographers. At one moment he was talking about us as though we were fictional characters, 'not particularly entertaining' he said, and then realised that if it was indeed a documentary he was making disobliging remarks like that about real people, who were sitting next to him, with strained smiles for the benefit of the studio cameras trundling around like Daleks. 'I think some of the blame for my confusion,' he said, 'must be laid at Martin Shy's door. I want to ask him, don't you think a line should be drawn between truth and fiction?'

'Yes, I think the line should be drawn,' Martin replied. 'I just don't know anyone I'd trust to draw it for me.'

'Can you draw it for yourself?'

Martin spread his hands from the wrists, and looked straight at the on-air camera. 'What kind of truth is it that is not *someone's* truth? Certainly, this was not an impersonal film. On the contrary, in the course of making it, Andrew and Lise and I have become good friends. I made no attempt to alienate myself from the subject – or, rather, took no risk of doing so. Because, if I had, I would have been telling the most outrageous lie of all, by suggesting that, despite all the choices I have been responsible for, all the important things I decided to leave out, and all the apparently trivial ones I kept in, plus the obvious fact that by my very intrusion with a camera into their lives I altered their situation, despite all that, am I to offer the result as some kind of identikit of these people? It's rather a question of offering a finger-print, a chosen part from which you may be able to reconstruct the whole. What grammarians would call a synecdoche.'

'Plato's shadow on the cave wall,' the critic added.

'Nothing so pretentious,' Martin corrected him. 'I am just telling a story, a deliberate fiction, because that is more honest than any attempt to show the truth neat. If I've failed, if no viewer has taken from it the faintest idea of what Lise and Andrew are really like, as they start their marriage and their careers, then at least I have not damaged their own subjective realities. They are still there, intact.'

'Andrew,' the interviewer asked, 'would you maintain that television is one of the big truths of our society, or one of the big lies?'

'It's unquestionably a gigantic truth,' Andrew answered. 'It's there. It works like psychiatry, it rein-forces the status quo, adjusts the patient – that is, the viewer – back to the norms.'

'What norms do you mean?' the critic asked.

'Ideology. Personality. Do not adjust your set. Let it adjust your head.'

'Right,' Martin cut in. 'What you and I and most of us might casually agree is normality just may be seen by some people, more innocent than us perhaps, as an ap-palling, insane fantasy. Whether television can ever take account of that, which I suppose would require some kind of perpetual self-criticism, is the question.'

As the question had been addressed to the camera, no one in the studio attempted to answer it, and the interviewer, to keep the heads talking, asked, 'So what are the implica-tions of that for someone in your position, Martin?'

'That so-called documentary films, in that event, ought to be considered as a version of surrealism. A demented, wasted world, calmly observed by the Cyclops eye of the camera.'

The interviewer asked, 'Just now you, Andrew, seemed to be complaining that television as a medium, irrespective of the message, is a social control, a very conservative one, and I gathered from your tone that you object to it on those grounds. It's fair to ask, I think, whether you felt like that before you agreed to do the film and, if so, why you did agree?'

'Is anyone still watching this, do you suppose?' Andrew asked him.

'We have to proceed on that assumption.'

'Okay. Well, I guess the obvious answer is that we wouldn't've stopped television in its tracks by refusing, and to agree promised to be an enlightening experience.'

'Lise,' the interviewer asked, 'was it enlightening?'

'Yes, of course it was, for us. Obviously I can't say whether it succeeded or failed for the people who watched it. But from my point of view the key thing is that it forced us into a position where we had to look very hard at many things about ourselves that we had taken for granted before.'

'Yes,' the critic nodded at her. 'I can see that. But one has seen the kind of programme that visibly changes its subject, by peeling illusions off them, in public, and one is bound to fear that if you succeed in stripping away people's life-lies, so to speak, they may find it difficult to go on living. But the self-examinations in this film were handled, I would say, with a tact which didn't threaten to damage you, as Martin Shy put it.'

The interviewer thanked them all, and hoped that the viewers would watch next week's film in this series about Starters, which would take a look at a young man who was in his first year as a student of theology. That was at 8.30, next Thursday, and until then, good night. When the picture had faded on the monitor, the interviewer thanked them all again, 'for real, I mean'.

'I hate it when people talk to me about my films,'

Martin said in the bar afterwards. 'It's as though they're saying, "Ah, now I see what you're up to." '

'You were very good,' the critic told him.

'Balls. All those things are a waste of time. They never leave room for accidents. Do you know the only thing in it that anyone will remember tomorrow? – when Andrew asked Charlie if anyone was still watching. That broke the rules, for a moment.'

'Notwithstanding,' the critic said, 'I think this company is going to miss you.'

'You hear that, Julia?' Martin asked his PA. 'You're going to miss me.'

'Do you think we'll miss him?' Julia asked Manny.

'Yes,' Manny said, 'he'll leave a strangely shaped gap that will be hard to fill.'

Andrew was too exhausted to join in the talk. He looked at Lise, who, quiet herself, seemed to be the lodestar of the table, to whom everyone else's attitude was addressed. He leaned to whisper in her ear, 'You are a very beautiful girl, and you're going to be a lovely mother.' Lise wrinkled her nose fondly at him. How perfectly her head and neck were poised upon her white collarbone.

It pierces him through, and through, that moment, remembered now in Martin's office, alone, at night, hurting each time no less than the first, a vulture at his liver.

He looks at the dossier on his lap. Has it really been worth it, worth the trouble of lying to Len in Reception that Martin had asked Andrew to fetch something from his office? What Lise had said to Martin in that low-lit studio seemed, as he read it through, to be a trail leading to what they had said to each other on those walks they took. But when the trail ran out, Andrew was still in the middle of the dark wood; the pages of words would not disclose the insights Lise had spoken of, nor the understanding with which Martin had coaxed them. If he could only have

78

heard the voices! And, for the present, he is compelled by a puritan scruple to recognise that he was no less curious to see just how his own transcripts had been edited in Martin's copy. 'I don't know what I am going to do,' he says aloud.

'Do?' Lise had answered, the evening after the film went out. 'There's nothing for you to do. Anyway, he's going away next week, to make this film in Jugoslavia, so you won't have anything to worry about then, will you?'

'Lise!' Andrew could see that the spite in her was at Martin, for going away, not at himself, for his jealousy when she told him she was off for another walk.

'Why don't you come too,' she said, 'and have it out with him?'

'Have what out?'

'Since you insist on your right to be jealous, despite all your hypocritical theories against women being sexual property.'

'So it is sexual.'

'You're twisting my words.'

'And you're twisting my balls. Off.'

'Before we got married, I used to believe everything you said. But you don't believe any of it, yourself.'

'True,' Andrew said to Ho Chi Minh as the door slammed behind her. 'My acts are widows of my dreams.'

What else could he do but drink, and what else could the drink do but transmute him, body and soul, to lead?

She came back, hours later, in tears. Half in a leaden sleep, he was moved by her distress, but she turned angrily away from his arm, and slept with her back to him. 'It's no good,' he smiled, 'I love your back, too.'

In the morning, she was in a calm depression. They lay side by side, and she told him that she had been to bed with Martin, last night. It was the first time. All the rest had been talking, truly. Andrew lay still, and did not say anything, for a long time. The sun was bright behind the curtains, and birds were singing. If he had not been jealous when it was only talking, perhaps it would not have gone past talking. Lise smoked a cigarette, slowly. 'It was awful,' she said.

'He was?'

'Yes. Poor thing.' She closed her eyes.

Andrew, eyes open, was looking for the first time at an image that would not leave him for months to come, of Martin penetrating Lise, her belly, pregnant, against his. That is the other moment, imagined this time, not remembered, that pierces him through, and through.

'It was my doing,' Lise said. 'I took him to bed. He never would have.'

'Why?' Andrew asked softly. 'Why, Lise?'

'I wanted to prove something to myself, I suppose.'

'Prove what?'

'I don't know.'

'Something you couldn't prove with me?'

'Yes, it must have been. I don't know. I thought it would be something quite new to me.'

'Where were you?'

'What? Oh, at his house. Sybil's away, with the kids, seeing her mother.'

Lise started to cry, quietly. Andrew put his arm around her, and she did not resist it, nor respond.

'If it had been all you hoped, what then?' Andrew asked, still softly, confused by tenderness and hatred cohabiting. The piercing images would not let him be. 'What of us, then? And the baby?'

'I don't know. I'd have had to talk to him about it.'

'To him?' Andrew spoke quickly for the first time. 'And me? Would I have had a say?'

'Of course you would.' Lise's crying was louder, and she turned away from him.

Andrew looked at her sobbing back. He found the tenderness had gone from him.

He got dressed, and took her a cup of coffee. She had stopped crying, and was smoking a second cigarette. 'It's supposed to be bad for the baby, smoking when you're pregnant,' he reproached her.

Lise's eyes, at him, under reddened lids, glared with plain dislike. 'I know,' she said, crushing the cigarette in the ashtray.

That day, both of them did the best, most concentrated work of all their rehearsals. The play was still much too romantic, Andrew knew, but he had given in. Walking home, through a sunset evening, he asked Lise, 'Is there any way out of this, for us?'

'It's all over,' Lise answered.

'Between you and him?'

'Yes.'

'And between us?'

'I don't know.'

'It is an agony that I'm living through, but if we can survive it, perhaps we will be stronger, at the broken places.'

'I don't know if I believe in marriage any more.'

'Marriage? Or being married to me?'

'Being married to you, I suppose. I don't know any other.'

That she could, now, pierce him so painfully, with an almost absent-minded skill, impressed Andrew. Martin's effect on her had been to temper her finely. He was nervous of her, for the first time. 'On those walks and talks you had with him,' he asked, 'he made you aware, I take it, of the reciprocal illusions that two people must have about each other if they decide they love each other enough to get married?'

'Something like that. No, not really—'

'What I was going to say was that when all the illusions have gone there may still be something left.'

'He just made me aware of parts of myself, possibilities in me, that I'd never really seen before.'

'And it's too soon, I guess, for you to judge whether, now you do know about them, they could develop with me?'

'Probably.'

Andrew's curiosity to know how Martin had spoken to Lise, to arouse that awareness in her, was intense. It was then that he decided to burgle Martin's files, hoping that the transcripts would offer some clues. As they walked on through the quiet evening, he found that his envy of Martin was, for a time, more powerful than his jealousy of Lise. The picture he formed of those talks they had had was one in which Martin, with that negative capability of his, had merely listened sympathetically, with an encouraging word now and then, while Lise had dredged out of herself all the new insights which she now attributed to him, gratefully. It was a con trick on his part, as glib as the learning and good living – so easily worn! like pre-faded jeans – which lend him his waterproof manner among the rest of us, who know failure, make ridiculous errors, and admit to them. But behind that dazzle there's a tin-plate fascist, with unspeakable terror gesticulating inside him. His systematic philosophy aims at perfect understanding as life aims at death. His terror is of chance, flux, what happens, just the accidents he delights to shoot on film, as though pinning wretched butterflies.

Poor Lise, so hoodwinked. If I had seen all this before, Andrew thought, I need not have smiled tolerantly while she persisted in it. But O! what a beautiful irony, what a perfectly formed bubble, that, when he for once put that dazzle at risk and dropped his trousers, the outcome was more awful – Lise's word – than any accident he could film. He laughed, and looked at Lise, but did not explain.

In the middle of the evening the door-bell rang. Andrew, in the bath, heard Lise go to answer it. Then there was a woman's voice, not Lise's, raised. Andrew could not hear the words because the water-tank was filling. The door was slammed. Andrew put a towel around himself, and went to find out what had happened. Lise was prostrate on the bed, biting a blanket. She would not turn to face him, so he walked around the bed and sat there. 'Who was that?' he asked. Still she didn't move her head, nor even her staring eyes, but she began to tremble. He was scared that hysteria might bring on a miscarriage. 'Lise, tell me, for God's sake. What's happened?'

In the end she told him. It had been Sybil. She had got Martin to drive her to the flat. He was waiting outside to drive her home again afterwards, Sybil had said.

'What was it she wanted to say to you?'

Lise bit the blanket, and didn't answer. Andrew stroked her hair, while she went on staring, rigid, trembling. 'I don't believe her,' he said.

'I do,' Lise said quickly. 'If he told her at once about him and me last night – he probably had to ring her at her mother's – why shouldn't he have done that, too?'

'Ring him, and ask him. I'll get him for you.'

'No! There's nothing else I want to hear him say.'

'What a 24-carat bastard.'

'No he's not. He's just weak. Strong professionally, but emotionally weak.'

'An evil combination.'

'Yes,' Lise agreed. Andrew could see her relaxing a little now, talking about it. 'She can't cope with his success,' Lise went on. 'He told me about all that. It's hard on him. But he'd never have the courage to leave her, and the kids.'

'Did you talk about it?'

'Not explicitly.'

Andrew realised then that he had allowed himself to forget what Lise had said the previous night, 'It was my doing.' His picture of the relationship had to be focussed again. Lise had wanted Martin to live with her, it

83

seemed – while she was carrying Andrew's baby. Before the bitterness could sear his words, he spoke again. 'You used to say that Martin understood you so well. Yet now you say he is weak.'

'That's not incompatible. Quite the reverse, in fact.'

Soon, Lise started to cry, and Andrew let her, stroking her hair still. Martin was a mystery to him once more. And that part of Lise which had communed with his mystery was, itself, mysterious.

When she went to sleep, Andrew dressed, and left to burgle Martin's filing-cabinet, but it didn't help.

Only her professional pride got Lise through the next few days of rehearsal. A word from Martin, even a weak word, would have helped her, but none came, and by now he would have left for Jugoslavia. Andrew was not in much better shape, but he knew that his ordeal was less than his wife's. At home he treated her as convalescent, and the authority of it fed his energy at work: that, and his reservoir of anger. Anger at whom? he asked himself, after each piercing image. At Martin, whose fictions, and fickle amity, had sapped the strength from Lise and himself, sucked them like Dracula? At Lise, who apparently had initiated the affair with Martin? At himself, for smiling and indulging her while she did it?

Tickets for *Romeo and Juliet* were selling unusually well for a drama school show, the Principal's secretary told them. 'A lot of people say they saw you in that tv programme.'

'Then they'll expect us to do Angelo and Isabella visit Verona,' Andrew said.

'But what about the agents, are they coming?' Lise wanted to know.

'Several have rung up for tickets,' the secretary said. 'Mind you, there were four of them here last year.'

'After the interval?' Andrew asked.

'Go on with you,' said the secretary, who enjoyed being joshed, 'just because you were only carrying a spear.'

'And this year I'm carrying the company.'

The secretary made big-head gestures at him, and went tittering off.

'Ironic, don't you think,' Andrew remarked to Lise, 'that they're going to pack the house to watch us do a highly romantic performance of *Romeo and Juliet* because of Martin?'

'I don't care why they come, so long as they come,' she said.

He didn't tell Lise that he was pierced by the penetrating image every day when he woke up, and often unawares. He was ashamed of his jealousy. It was as she had said, just sexual imperialism. Slowly, with the work to distract them, they might piece it all together again. As the baby in her grew, the strength to forgive her could grow in him.

He did the cooking, the shopping, and cleaning, and did not complain that she sat and watched him, or didn't watch him but just stared at things. He took her out to eat, at little Italian places, proud to see heads turn for her, but they ate without talking. Any direct enquiry from him about what preoccupied her, and offer to talk it over or do something to help her, she answered with a slow shake of her head, and sometimes a little smile. She went to bed early, but was always awake before him, and several times, waking up in the middle of the night, he would know from her breathing that she was awake, too. He said she ought to go to see the doctor; she shook her head.

Then, on the Saturday morning a week after the crisis, she was bright in her face again. She was going home for the weekend, she said, and Monday too. The director had agreed to schedule rehearsals accordingly.

'I'll come with you, till tomorrow evening,' Andrew said.

'No, I'd rather go on my own.'

'Why? I'd like to come.'

'It will be a weekend with my family like it used to be. That's what I feel would do me a lot of good. If you were there, it would be different, a visit.'

'I distrust all that. It's as though you're retreating from reality into a cosy fantasy of the past.'

'Perhaps I am. But only for a weekend, Andrew. That can't be bad, can it?'

So bright she looked, childlike, that he hadn't the heart to deny her a treat; still less to sneer, as the old serpent in him wanted to, 'So we re-hang the door. When the going gets tough, we fall back into the ever-loving arms of Daddy's expensive armchair.'

She went, in her car, and Andrew spent the weekend at the cinema, walking about the city, reading two Sunday papers, and just watching the fears and hopes chase each other around the Grecian urn of his head. He missed her much more than he had expected. The little death with her was nothing in comparison to the great death it would be without her, wrinkling her nose fondly.

On Monday evening, after a long day rehearsing, he found Lise already back in the flat. The brightness had fallen from her. She looked tired again. He spoke politely, waiting to know what virus of thought her parents' home might have implanted in her. Soon, she turned to him and said, 'I've had an abortion.' It was a challenge, the way she spoke the words. In her eyes he saw fear, of him, her husband.

He asked her carefully, 'Do you mean you've paid to have the operation done?'

'Yes. To be exact, my father paid for it.'

'Your father. He thought it was a good idea, then.'

'He saw it was the only thing to do, when I told him about everything else. My mother agreed, too.'

'I expect your great-aunt twice removed would have agreed, as well. But probably you didn't ask her.'

Lise just went on watching him.

'I really must get myself registered in Debrett's,' Andrew said, 'so that people will ask me, when there's a question of murdering my child.'

'I knew you'd feel bitter,' Lise said.

'How well you know me.'

'I knew it would be yourself you were sorry for, without thinking of me, how much I needed to do it.'

'How much did you need, a hundred and fifty?' Andrew answered. The fear had left Lise's eyes. Perhaps it hadn't been fear. 'Or maybe more?' Andrew wondered. 'I expect your father knew the very best man to go to, somewhere in Surrey. Tell me, was that the county where my child was chucked in a waste bin? I'd be glad to know.'

The imagined child for whom he grieved was not, in fact, a small baby but an infant boy, enjoying a run with him through flowers, shrieking, tumbling, being picked up and swung high on straight arms. As an image, it had the advantage of being strong enough to blot out, for some weeks to come, the others that had been piercing him through.

Lise had walked from the sitting-room into the bedroom. Andrew stood still, his eyes closed. Then he followed her, and stood in the doorway, watching her unpack a suitcase. He said, 'As I expect this will be the last time we speak to each other as man and wife, as opposed to Romeo and Juliet, and rival plaintiffs in court, there are some things I want to tell you. The first is that I loved you so much that I shall cry whenever I remember it.'

'You never loved me,' Lise interrupted him.

'No?'

'You're too self-contained to love. You thought you did. I'm not saying you're a liar. But that wasn't love.'

'Nor in you for me?'

Lise stopped unpacking for a second, shrugged, and went on.

'Nasty one, wasn't it?' Andrew observed. 'A sort of Catch-22. Or perhaps more like a snake on the winning square.'

Lise started to undress. Andrew watched her, and said, 'I should warn you that I feel like fucking you to death, quite literally, and I believe a man cannot be held to have raped his wife. Which is a good job, since rape is what it usually felt like with you, if not necrophily.'

'You're not staying here tonight,' Lise told him.

'I thought you might consent to my using my own sofa.'

'I'd rather you went somewhere else.'

'No, I suspect some legal tactic here, figured out with Daddy.'

'I shall lock that door.'

'As you please.'

'You don't mind if I get into bed, then, while you're finishing your speech? I was told to rest as much as possible. Incidentally, if you do rape me, it's quite likely that it would kill me.'

Killing Lise, or himself, or both, were scenes that Andrew watched that night, behind his eyes, open in the darkness. By morning light he had composed a couplet to be inserted in Romeo's lament over the body of Juliet, thus:

> How oft when men are at the point of death
> Have they been merry? which their keepers call
> A lightning before death: O, how may I
> Call this a lightning? O my love! my wife!
> Thou'rt plainly a lady, by the way thou look'd
> Wanking wi' thy little finger crook'd.
> Death, that hath suckt the honey, &c

Two

I expect you've guessed that the whole book so far was written by Andrew himself. *The Autobiography of a Drowning Man*, he thought of calling it, *or, In The Destructive Element Immersed*. He wanted to understand it all: that last, superstitiously revered relic of the Age of Reason – I shall understand, therefore I will not suffer. By noting down the 'narrative line' he hoped he might gradually 'trace' what he called 'the subtext'. In the third person, he would be more 'objective'. (Yes, the inverted commas stab their ironies in like a fleet banderillero, but be careful whom you mock, mon semblable.) He soon got on to the dossier of transcripts he'd taken from Martin's office, and wondered if copying them out in his own hand, word by word, could unravel anagrams he'd missed in reading them through. But it didn't, as he has said more than once. Finally, he thought he might as well complete the job by setting down what he could remember of the conversations; and that served, at least, to anaesthetise some of the pain. In fact, reading the conversations through yet again, on one of his sunnier days, several months after he'd written them down, he imagined what a nice two-hander a dramatist might make of them, for Lise and himself to do. He wrote Lise a chirpy note about it, but never posted it to her. It went into the file with all the others. He read them most nights, and sometimes improved a phrase or two.

He lived in, and seldom left, a room on the first floor of

the commune where they had filmed. In one corner, on the bare planks, was a mattress with some blankets; elsewhere, a table and chair, a gramophone, and a tea-chest, no other furniture. The wallpaper was dirty white, and in the dusk receded. He had some clothes in the tea-chest, and at the bottom was a bottle of Lise's scent, that he took out and sniffed when he read his letters to her, and at other times. Also, he had a pair of her shoes in there, but they weren't, whatever you think, a kinky remembrance of her, not much of that anyway, but had more to do with his mother, because they resembled (fashion being the whirligig it is) a pair, white, high-heeled, glossy, that he remembered finding, in a cupboard at home, when he was a small child. He had told Lise that when she'd bought them. Your mother's feet loom large in your infancy.

The sun shone through the uncurtained window of his room in the afternoons, travelling its bright stain across the wooden planks and up the wallpaper, and he was grateful to be in the commune. The Romeo couplet had dished him at the drama school. Probably he wouldn't have spoken it but for the presence in the last-night audience of Manny, which touched Andrew, and also gave him the hope that Manny might one day see Martin again, and report to him what the large audience had heard. 'Didn't you know,' the Principal had reproached him in a voice like Wolfit's, 'there were *agents* in tonight?' Now Andrew couldn't think of anything he wanted to do, nor anywhere else to go, outside the city where Lise was. She had got two girls from the school to join her in the flat, and had changed the lock. All unnecessary, Andrew had told her through the letter-box, he was going quietly. She wouldn't even let him in to collect the few things he was taking with him, but told him to write out a list and put it through the letter-box, and she would leave the stuff on the landing for him, outside the door, that evening. Andrew posted the list in to her, and walked round to the bank to clear out their joint account, not feeling too badly about that, since he had left her so much of their joint property in the flat, and anyway Daddy would replenish her, and bat no lid. He let the stuff stand on the landing several days before he collected it.

The money would see him through months in the commune. There was no rent or rates to pay; the commune was a squat in a house that belonged to the council, who intended to demolish it, and meanwhile refused to take rent in order to protect their legal possession, but did not harass the squatters, nor disconnect the mains supplies. Six pounds a week each into the communal fund paid for food, bought from a macrobiotic shop in the next street, and cooked, when it was cooked, on an old Belling plate by the girl with the baby. She lived free, in return. The fund also paid for such electricity as a few light-bulbs, the Belling, and gramophones used. The taps still ran with water, chilly evenings could be cheered in the communal room by a fire built from city jetsam, and Andrew counted his blessings, punctiliously, always concluding, 'Bring us not, Lord, very low'. It was not that his faith had settled upon him again, no, just that the old slogans stick, don't they?, Cardinal Newman's no less than J. Walter Thompson's. And that one in particular stuck, because Andrew heard it most days, playing, as he did, nothing on his gramophone but Elgar. A choice between apostles was something he thought it best to defer, till he was strong once more. For now, he leaned trustingly against the marble pillars of Elgar, wreathed in weeds, not only the *Dream of Gerontius* but also both symphonies and both concertoes. Upstairs, Bad-Feet Willie seldom played anything but the three records of *Turandot*. The rest of the house was wanton, flipping from Zappa to Palestrina and on to Messiaen with an infidelity that Andrew did not envy. Nor did he envy Bad-Feet Willie his Puccini. 'It's too easy,' he told him. Willie giggled, and said it wasn't easy too, there were the riddles, and anyway he never played the last side.

Also upstairs, in the room facing Willie's, lived Julian, plump and dark as a plum, and juicy. He was a tyrannical lover to Willie, tormenting him after two nights of sweetness by bringing home a boy or a girl, for a night, maybe a week, then booting them out again and kissing the tears off Willie's face. 'How can he do it to me?' Willie would complain. 'With my feet, *I* can't piss off, he knows that, the Satan.' And the others knew that Willie's lament, though played for laughs, was not affected. He loved Julian truly, had brought him into the commune hoping to settle down with him, and cried himself to sleep every time Julian betrayed him. But to remonstrate with Julian was useless. 'I contain multitudes,' he answered quietly, closing his brown eyes, 'so how can Willie ever contain me?'

In the room below Andrew's lived the quiet mother, Emma, with her baby, whom everyone called Sundance. They seemed a self-sufficient couple, though some nights a man, presumably Sundance's father, stayed with them. He was a married man, Andrew learned, but Emma was too shy, or too sad behind her placid smile, to say any more about him. She shopped, and cooked, and sometimes offered to take washing to the laundrette, and in an evening around the fire she would sing folksongs to them, plucking a few basic chords on her guitar, with the air of one who is looking for a voice mislaid somewhere on the journey, and meanwhile has only this frail one to apologise with. Her shyness irritated Andrew. It seemed a sort of complacency.

The other two communards, in the room facing Andrew's, were the aggressive dark-haired girl and the man who had spoken about Anarchism, when the film crew had visited. Diana and Pete. It was they who had consented to let Andrew live in the empty room of the house

94

(the previous occupant had been a girl who cleared out one evening with not a trace left behind) when, like a broken bird, he had tapped on the front door. 'Have you got somewhere I could live?'

'This is a commune, not a hotel,' Diana answered.

'I'd like to join.'

'Where's your wife?'

'She's not, any more. Nothing is, any more. I'm on my own, now.'

No wife, no baby, no acting, no film crew, he told them, but they were suspicious. Still, they let him have the room. Thank you, sweet Jesus, it was a perfectly empty space, a tabula rasa, for starting again, starting over, and out.

I haven't been outside for maybe two months, but the best of it is, the outside hasn't been in. Have the White Russians issued from Bayswater and secured their counter-coup across the frozen Neva? Have world parities been tied to the Dope Standard? Has David Bowie achieved parthenogenesis? I might like to hear, one day, one smoky autumn day when I have ceased to dance, finally, and the tidal wave of earth has quite covered over all traces of what men have done while their eyes were bloodshot with Reason. Here comes the sun. For now, the question that more closely nuzzles me for an answer is: that man poised above the dark street outside my window, thoughtfully sucking a fag as he stares in at me from the night—is he my biographer? or my murderer? And another question, o my love, what viciously giggling god was it who wet his pants when he came up with the scenario that I need you like water, but you, like water, can ripple along fine with no need of this drinker? Get me that god's emerald eyes, set them in a bracelet, and shackle it to a goat's ankle, Andrew wrote, and filed it with the rest.

Diana and Pete tolerated him, no more. He did his share of the communal tasks, but went back up to his room afterwards. 'The idea,' Diana told him, 'is we share our experiences, and feelings, too.'

'All mine have turned into demons,' Andrew replied. 'If I commanded them to give the rest of you a fair turn on the spit, they'd cackle.'

'We might be able to help you through it,' she said. 'Like on a trip.'

'Maybe when I'm coming up. I'm still howling vertically down, like a bomb.'

'But we could authenticate it, the madness you've got to get through. You could try it, at least. Trust us.'

'I can't,' Andrew said, walking upstairs.

It was as though his brain had shrunk a little inside his skull, withdrawing his eyes with it, on their fibrous strings. Soon he would be able to look down the well of his own body. Down to the root. If he could get it right there, he would strip off the layers, fat years and lean, throw away everything he could do without, and emerge precisely and economically as himself.

Perhaps, he thought, mixing himself another metaphor, the trick was to re-enact every passage of his life that seemed to have been formative, but with a negative charge to cancel each one out, as a typist goes over errors with a white carbon. Knowing – like you, mon semblable, so defended inside your musculature – knowing that the idea was steam from an overheated cerebral cortex, he nevertheless had nothing better to do than experiment by singing early Beatles songs on a monotone, thinking that a period of such innocence and promise would be easily cancelled, in rehearsal for the tougher tracks of his days with Lise, with his father at home, the misguidance of his schooldays, the boyhood books – *Eric, The Adventures of a Penny, Coral Island, The Swiss Family Robinson*, Kingsley's *Heroes* – and, ultimately, what shapes he might dredge up from the fine silt of his infancy. But even the monotone set up columns of resonance. For one thing, it soon sounded like Gregorian chant, reminding him of a morning when his father, after their bible-reading, had prayed that his son be not tempted by the allurements of the Catholic Church.

Andrew saw his face staring hopelessly at him from the dark windowpane, smiled, and absconded from the experiment. The obvious and sane task, he decided, was to scrutinise his life as objectively as he could, noting how each successive stage complicated all that had gone before, and unpick the pattern, backwards. Oh, what a tangled web we weave, when we believe that we believe. Only when that work was completed, and understood, could he 'formulate', he said aloud, 'an antithesis to raise my consciousness of myself dialectically'. So he rested, finally, on the image of looking down inside himself.

Curled up on his mattress, eyes closed for concentration, he found that his mind insisted on a direct shuttle service between Lise and his mother. 'At an early age,' he said, 'I learned that the intense moments of my life would be those that are beautiful and tragic, both.' A full minute passed before he shouted 'Oh hell,' and paced the diagonals of the room. It was ridiculous. The palpable absence of Lise and the figments he had of his mother were linked by nothing at all save the sentimental fictions of Freud. You might as well try to explain starvation in Bangladesh by a reading of the Greek myths. Or the Old Testament, come to that. *'Who is as the wise man?'* Andrew recited, *'and who knoweth the interpretation of a thing?* Who knoweth why Lise, Lise, Lise left me? I've not even started to understand that.' Later, he might, but only by first knowing himself.

Down to the root. What would it have been like if his mother had lived, who would he be? Sitting at his table, he invented conversations with her, as he imagined her. He thought how he might kiss her: on the cheek, the forehead, the hair? To be his mother's son – he couldn't imagine it, except in stereotypes that he recognised for what they were. He longed to know. With his hand across his eyes, he ached for the life he had not had. That love depleted. How sad she must have been to die and leave her baby. On her deathbed she had given his father a penny, and whispered, 'That's to give Andrew.' His father, telling him that, had admitted that he had not kept the coin. Thank God, it would have been like radium to touch.

It was all so incredibly long ago. Andrew was nearly her age, now, and she still wore the post-war A-line frock. His imagination couldn't dress her differently, nor paint age on her face. His father looked forward to seeing his wife again in heaven, but even in his piety Andrew had always rejected that, with an anger he concealed. *Say not thou, What is the cause that the former days were better than these? for thou dost not enquire wisely.* He lit a cigarette. It was after midnight, but Bad-Feet Willie would be awake. As Andrew stood up, he knocked the glass ashtray from the table, spilling it on the floor.

Willie was in bed, wearing green silk pyjamas, and a white silk scarf around his neck. Julian, elegant in a brown suit, the waistcoat crossed by two gold chains, one to a watch, the other to a pendant opal, was seated astride a chair, reading aloud from Rochester. 'Do you mind if I listen?' Andrew asked. Julian waved him to a low, wooden-armed chair, but shut the book. 'Do go on,' Andrew said.

Julian shook his head, and stroked his Macmillan moustache with a finger. 'You're an actor,' he said. 'I'd like to be an actor, so I'm not going to parade my shortcomings with you watching.'

Andrew told him, 'You could be a good actor.' Julian smiled at him, his large eyes saying, Don't you patronise me. 'You know how to use silence,' Andrew went on. 'For instance, you know how to pause, when you're speaking, in such a way that no one will interrupt you.'

'I have presence, you mean?'

'Call it that.'

'Are you listening, Willie?' Julian asked. 'I have presence, did you know?'

'Yes,' Willie said. 'Absence is what I've got.'

Julian ruffled Willie's hair, and meanwhile looked up at Andrew. 'Would you read to us?'

Now Andrew shook his head. 'No. I'm not an actor, any more.'

'Just read one thing, for us,' Willie asked him.

Andrew picked a book at random from a shelf. *Collected Poems* by Robert Graves. He let it fall open at any page.

'I think that's about the sixth *Collected Poems* he brought out,' Julian remarked. 'Here once again are the main points of the Muse, I call it.'

Andrew was gazing at the page. The title of the poem was *Leda*:

> And there beneath your god awhile
> You strained and gulped your beastliest.
>
> Pregnant you are, as Leda was,
> Of bawdry, murder and deceit . . .

He shut his eyes, then the book. It looked as if he was about to recite from memory. He breathed in, and shut his mouth. Julian and Willie waited. 'I'm sorry,' Andrew said, 'I can't. It just happened to open at a poem that throws me. I can't read it.'

Bad-Feet Willie sucked his lower lip, and nodded slowly. 'The certainty of hazard,' he observed.

Andrew answered, 'Balls is what I'd like to say to that, but I don't feel able to, at the moment.'

'Don't you believe in revelation?' Willie was surprised.

99

'Not that kind. Not any kind of revelation, any more. Maybe.'

'Ah,' Julian said, 'you're a man of the Enlightenment. Reason shall prevail.'

Willie was still truly surprised. 'You don't throw the I Ching ever? Or consult the ouija board?'

Andrew looked away, shaking his head. 'No. Never.'

'With that much faith in reason,' Julian said to Willie, 'he must be a Libra.'

'With Sagittarius in the ascendant,' Willie agreed.

Andrew was standing in a corner. 'I don't know what I think about reason,' he said, 'but I hate all that stuff. You must forgive me. I used to be a Christian.'

'The nail is in the other foot, I'd have thought,' Julian answered.

'I've lost it,' Andrew went on, 'but I haven't lost my respect for it, over all the pathetic little dribbles of superstition that people make do with, instead.'

'Pathetic is right, Willie,' Julian said.

'Right on,' Willie answered.

'I don't expect you to take me seriously,' Andrew said. 'I don't even specially want you to.'

'Oh come on, already,' Julian reproached him. 'It's you who're playing at fallen angels, so we're stooging for you as some smaller fry of demon. Don't be like that. No one likes a paranoiac. This is a commune, remember. Mutual aid, and that.'

'You're cynical about that, too, then?' Andrew asked.

'I thought you put your finger on the nipple in that television programme.'

'Don't remind me.'

'The people downstairs think that Anarchism is an ego-trip around the Statue of Liberty. Willie and I beg to differ. At least, Willie begs. I just take. So what if they do get to be the folks on the idyll, and no one's into property, or orders? That's just a nice time for themselves, another version of property. And they'll gradually compromise, you know they will, until in the end they'll be utterly tolerated, assimilated, which is just another way of obeying orders. Nothing will have been changed. Nothing. I'm too attached to my balls, or they're too attached to me, to let them be ever so gently sliced off like that. So is Willie, aren't you?'

'I do admire his gift of ambiguity, don't you?' Willie asked Andrew.

'What's your alternative?' Andrew asked Julian.

'To act.'

'To act against the way it is?'

'Right.'

'Not stopping short of violence?'

'Preferably not. It's quicker, and surer.'

'Also, people get hurt.'

'Also, people already get hurt.'

'True. I got hurt recently, when my wife left me. The reasons why she did that were complex, but you could roughly call them social.' Andrew sat down, looked at the other two, and smiled. 'I'm in a bad way.'

'You agree with us, then?' Julian asked him.

'That it is necessary to act, yes.'

'But not violently?'

'No. There's always a random fall-out. The wrong people suffer.'

'They're all collaborators.'

'No, that's too easy. There are the exploiters, and the exploited.'

'And everybody is both. Bugger exploitation. Randomness is the principle we live by.'

'You and Willie, you mean? Or everyone?'

'Everyone in the world.' Julian was standing by the straight-backed chair now, leaning his right elbow on it and gesturing with his left. He looked like a successful Peruvian, but his voice had the mocking edge and high registers that are taught in public schools. 'As a Christian, you must have believed in fate. As a Marxist too, come to that.'

'On the contrary . . .'

'You had faith,' Julian said, 'right? That means, you trusted in some system, some providence, which you couldn't know, for yourself, but which was going to resolve the meaning of your life. So, you believed in a destiny, of sorts, a fate. Your personal responsibility, as you'd call it, was only an ethic, for everyday behaviour, like a railway timetable. It didn't make any difference to where the train was going.'

'Some people can know God, or providence, or dialectical materialism, or whatever word you use. I have to admit I never did.'

'Some people *call* it that,' Julian answered. 'They've got to call the experience something. Why not call it, let's say, the exhilaration of feeling, for a moment, that you are the focal point of a random, shifting field of cosmic energy? A bit more wordy than God, but it will serve. Now, where is the personal responsibility in that?'

Andrew massaged the inner corners of his eyes. 'I came up here to get away from questions,' he smiled. 'I suppose a change of questions is as good as a solution. Is it always like this in here – the Higher Chamber?'

'We don't get many visitors who come here to talk,' Willie answered.

Julian was stroking his moustache, and watching the floor. Now he looked up again. 'What's your answer?' he asked, and waited.

'In one respect I'm in agreement with you. The concept of personality has got to be destroyed. What we need is archetypes, and rituals—'

'Rituals,' Julian affirmed, cutting in. 'Collective identities. Anonymity. That way, we work along the grain of fate. So the question is, how do we proceed,

102

from here, in practical terms? What are we going to *do*?'

'It can be like that in a theatre,' Andrew said, 'collective, and anonymous. It's what the theatre was for, in ancient Greece.'

'But now we have to create our own theatres,' Julian said, 'and the quickest means is an act of violence. It immediately defines the place it happens in as a theatre. The people who witness it are exhilarated by the freedom they feel. They are grateful to the actors. And the actors have generated a spiritual energy so intense that it may, just, influence the cosmic field. *That* is what I call our responsibility. Our duty, if you like.'

'If you feel like that, what are you doing living in this set-up?'

Willie answered, 'We like it here. We're on the edge of things. No one bothers us. We've got time to answer all these riddles.'

Julian murmured, 'There's no riddle.'

'But,' Andrew said, 'from the others, downstairs, I gathered the commune was a pacifist alternative, a nice time for themselves, as you put it. If you said "violence" to them, they'd think you were talking about ICI chemicals.'

'We don't have much to do with them,' Willie said, 'apart from eating.'

'So it's really not a proper commune at all? No community of thought, or feeling? I mean, you don't have arguments like this with them, but against them?'

'They know what we think of them and their dreary, middle-class anxieties,' Julian said.

'I didn't understand any of this when we were doing the filming here,' Andrew said. 'Where were you?'

'Up here,' Willie said, 'smoking.'

'While they were doing what they knew the film cameras wanted,' Julian added.

'Why do they let you stay?'

'We were in before they could suss us out,' Bad-Feet Willie smiled.

'Willie came in soon after they did,' Julian went on, 'and I joined him after that. The place doesn't belong to them. Anyway, it would blow all their philosophical circuits if they tried to hustle us out.'

Willie added, 'They need someone living up here to justify the squat, and I don't think they've got any like-minded friends who fancy it.'

'You know what they said about you, after that television programme?' Julian asked. 'That you were like all the other actors, trying to colonise our brains.'

Andrew, in his own room, turned the Elgar up loud, and started to write. *From the moment when you first told me you loved me, from that moment in that evening in your old flat, up all those stairs, Abbey Road turning and turning, I have been so entirely built on you that now, without you, my life is without meaning, a nonsense, an anacoluthon, a sentence with no main verb. If I am to go on at all, I have to reconstruct it, accepting the painful necessity of throwing out much that is dear to me but belongs to a different sentence. Also, it may be, the necessity of delving deeper still, into the foundations on which I erected what proved to be false premises, structures of cancer. I cannot risk having to live through all this again, even as comedy.*

It might have helped me if you had told me the whole story of what sundered us. But I think—hope—I can piece it together from the pattern of the tears remembered on your face.

There must be a pattern: to be understood, and accepted, the meanings ploughed back in, just as his father spoke of that cancer that had knotted his mother's breast as a figure in God's design.

Well, let the pattern reveal itself. Andrew tore up that

letter, and the rest before and after it in the file, noticing that his handwriting had grown smaller lately. He threw the confetti into the dustbin, along with the scent and the shoes. He painted his room black, walls, floor and ceiling black, and bought himself black clothes. He was ashamed of the wasted months. It was an impossible arrogance, a carrion comfort, to imagine that all the fluid world's problems might be accommodated in a sufficiently elaborate diagram. The only hope was to make sense for himself, abandoning reflection for action. By existing in a style with edges sharp as cut glass, one might become a prism through which the worried questions would refract themselves, and be resolved into the pattern of their primary colours. So be it.

He carried his head high. It felt light, as though his cranium had been emptied, a fat, overfed snail extruded from its shell. I'm out of that stiff neck of the woods, he said. It's futures I'm dealing in now.

To exorcise the ghosts, he invited Julian and Bad-Feet Willie down to his black room for a long night of drinking. He told them about Lise, and Martin, about his father and dead mother. It reminded him of the wildtrack recordings. When they were very drunk, they made a lot of noise. Pete came in to complain, but saw that it was useless. Andrew was declaiming Romeo's speeches to Bad-Feet Willie, while Julian, on the table, was pretending that his prick was a spotlight.

'Oh, Pete,' Julian shouted, 'you're so cool, calm, and collective.'

The next day, Diana told them that she and Pete were leaving. 'It's not just because of last night. We'd already decided that some time we want to get it together and make a commune in the country. We don't know where, yet. But last night, we realised that we've got to split now, wherever. We're just not into the same thing, all of us. Pete and I define Anarchism as the most self-disciplined experience you can have, with other people. You others – not Emma – seem to define it as a trip with no rules, no respect for other people, not even any interest at all in sharing your lives with ours. It's turned into one long downer for us, so that's it, we'll split tomorrow.'

'How about you, Emma?' Andrew asked.

'I'd like to stay on here,' she said.

'You know you kept Sundance awake all last night?' Diana asked them.

'You should have brought her up to join in the party,' Willie told Emma, who smiled, and said nothing.

'It was a very spontaneous party,' Julian told Diana. 'I thought spontaneity was a virtue, in your eyes.'

'Not when it's aggressive,' she said.

'What should we do with our aggression, then?'

'Suss out the contradictions in yourself that cause it,' Pete answered.

'You mean, adjust myself to the social order,' Julian said.

'No, adjust yourself to your own order.'

Julian shook his head. 'The trouble with all you liberals, whatever label you give yourselves, is that you can never see that conflict is necessary.'

'Come on, Pete,' Diana said. 'In nearly a year we haven't got it together as a commune here. We're not going to get anywhere now just by rapping on with them.'

In his new clothes, beneath his dark, Celtic face, Andrew was a handsome figure. A touch too austere, Julian and Bad-Feet Willie thought. 'I'll make a pendant for you,' Julian offered. 'That will do the trick.'

He invited Andrew into his room. There was a little bench, with a butane bunsen, a small vice and a neatly arranged rack of silversmith's tools, some strips of silver, and a filigree jar containing semi-precious stones, rings, medallions, and other ornaments. Hanging from hooks on the wall were a dozen fine-linked chains, mostly factory-made, but Julian took a silver chain that he had made himself, he said, and from the jar he chose the pendant ornament that he wanted to give to Andrew. It was a seven-sided silver coin, the size of a florin, with a hole through the centre. The engraved design was too worn to be deciphered. 'Ottoman, I think,' Julian said. 'It's pure silver, anyway.' He threaded the chain through the little ring already affixed to the coin, put it around Andrew's neck, and stood back to admire it.

'It's beautiful,' Andrew said. 'Mayn't I pay you for the silver?'

Julian, gazing at the pendant, slowly shook his head. 'I wouldn't want to transform a gift into cash. When I sell them, the more ordinary things, I get what's known as the reasonable market price. What's that got to do with value? Or virtue? How can it be reasoned? They're all alchemists, the money men, the bankers and credit houses, if they could only see it. In return for your time, and skill, and virtue, they dish out these rather ugly little bits of paper, and tell you that you can exchange it for someone else's time, skill and virtue, or, most wondrous of all, if you plant it in their safes it will grow! Did you know that the parity of silver to gold has been at 13½ to 1 since the Middle Ages, and that that happens to be the ratio of the moon's cycles to the sun's? And they think of themselves as rational men! I piss on their cash. All gold is fool's gold, when you let yourself believe that it can be transformed into something else. Shall I tell you what I love to do with cash? No, I'll show you. Come.'

Andrew followed Julian out of the house and along the streets, until they entered a betting shop. A dozen men and one old woman were in there, some gazing at the *Sporting Life* sheets pinned up, others sitting at tables, smoking, or picking their teeth. A loudspeaker was reporting results, price movements, and running. Behind the grilled counter, two equestrian prints, gone tatty at the edges, were drawing-pinned to the wall, like prints of the Virgin in a brothel.

Julian took a slip from a dispenser, glanced at the board prices, and wrote out a bet: *£2 win, Randy Brandy, 3.45 Devon and Exeter*. A few minutes later, the horse passed the post first, but was placed second to Flydal, after a stewards' enquiry had established that it had taken the latter's ground over the final flight. 'Marvellous,' Julian said. 'You see?' He was cackling with laughter, a sound so profane in that place that the manager asked him to stop. Julian couldn't, so they walked back home, across waste ground.

The point that Julian had paid to make he now put to Andrew with the eagerness of a Jehovah's witness on the doorstep. 'In this unholy, determinist-scientific-materialist culture we inhabit, prophecy, as George Eliot said, is the most gratuitous form of error. Exactly! It arouses fate from its superannuated slumber, on downers dished out by Karl Marx. Gratuitous prophecy has got a great future. We've got to poke that old dog fate in the ribs, make her frisk around a bit, and what better way to do it than by using the very grail of our culture, cash? When you make a bet, you are provoking luck to occur. Good luck or bad, it doesn't matter, you've forced fate to wake up and give your god-awful will a rest. You can switch off the engines, and let the winds blow your ego around the globe. And the beauty of it is that what you are losing or redeeming is time. Money is congealed time. Why the burgesses have always held gambling to be a sin is because it upsets their notions of linear time, you know? Holy Mother Growth, and St Progress. In an afternoon you can lose ten years of history, or win twenty of futurity. I've travelled beyond both ends of my life, in my time, and laughed each way, black in the face. I expect you know that even your old Archbishop Ramsey is addicted to playing Patience? Decaffeinated gambling, that's all, bless him.'

'Where do you get all this?' Andrew asked him.

'Betting on horses? At school, of course. I was the house bookmaker. But I prefer to be on the punting end, now. Have you ever been racing?'

'No. My father brought me up to look on gambling as sinful, as you said.'

'I'll take you and Willie to Royal Ascot, if you'd like.'

Why was Julian kind to him? Andrew wondered. The angle of Julian's head was always slightly held back, as though everything he said was calculated to produce an effect, that he wished to observe. It was ambiguous, waiting for Andrew to lead or be led. On what mission?

'You know what Arthur Koestler says,' Julian was quoting as they entered the house. 'Chance, he said, not causality, is the principle of physics nowadays. You might say that necessity is the abortionist of invention.'

Andrew shut his eyes in a pain that took him quite by surprise. 'You might,' he answered. 'Excuse me.'

He went into his room, shut the door, and lay down on the mattress. It was like a face outside the window, waiting for the curtains to be unsuspectingly drawn, that image of his unborn son, tumbling in flowers. He cried, deeply, the first time for weeks. Afterwards, as the drying tears tautened his cheeks, he was surprised again, staring at the black ceiling, at the cruelty that followed in his feelings. Not an undirected destructive cruelty, nor a hatred for Lise in particular, but a demand on him to be elegant, composed, ruthless. The scene that approximated to what he felt was one in which he coldly slew his opponent in a duel. The pistols, and frocks coats, suggested that the duel took place in early nineteenth-century Paris. Or Baden-Baden. Or maybe it was six shells ripping into a mattress.

He decided to test himself by doing what he had been most nervous of, calling on Lise.

One of her flatmates answered the door. He explained that he had come to collect his mail. She left him while he sorted through the letters in the hall. Before he had finished, Lise came out to see him. She was less beautiful than he expected. It made it easier.

He accepted a cup of coffee, but did not sit down. The sitting-room furniture had been switched around, and some pencil sketches by one of the girls were pinned up where the posters had been. He asked Lise what she was doing at the school. Eurydice, she said, in a treatment of the Orpheus myth which they were doing by improvisation.

'Shall I come and see it?' Andrew asked.

'We're not doing any public performances. It's just exercises.'

'Ah.'

'What are you doing?'

Andrew hesitated, and covered it by sipping his coffee. 'Nothing,' he said.

'That must be tiring.'

'It is, in fact.'

'Have you tried to get anything?'

'What sort of thing?'

'A job. Acting, somewhere.'

'No. I've given up the whole idea.'

She was less beautiful, but her legs, moving under her skirt, disturbed him. She sensed it, too, deliberately not tugging the skirt down the prim inch she normally would. But there was no question of an invitation in it: scorn, rather, or taunting, or perhaps just checking it out to make sure it all worked still.

'Have you got a lover?' he asked her.

'No. Not that it's any business of yours. Have you?'

'No.'

They avoided each other's eyes. A look would be as good as an admission, and neither would be sure what was being admitted. Andrew knew that a little lust was all he felt. He decided not to ask if she felt the same, because, were she to say yes, the sequel would be a proposition that they go to bed like strangers who do not know each other's name, and he found the subjunctive idea too attractive to risk.

'No,' he said, 'I don't know where my next wife is coming from.'

'You haven't got rid of this one, yet.'

'I imagine your family has the proceedings in hand.'

'Yes.'

'Have you heard from Martin?'

'I had a postcard from Dubrovnik.'

'If I asked what he said, would you tell me?'

'He told me to ring his agent.'

'Did you?'

'Yes. There's a chance of doing a television when I've finished here at the school.'

'With Martin?'

'No. He's not doing any television now.'

'It was just an intro, then?'

'He asked a producer to consider me for a part in a series.'

'Have you seen him, the producer?'

'Not yet.'

'The remorse of Martin Shy, is that the series?'

'I shouldn't think he's remorseful, just sad it didn't work out.'

'Like you.'

'I feel sorry for him, really. I'm not bitter. It must be awful to be married to Sybil.'

As Andrew started to leave, Lise said, 'I'll admit that part of the attraction in Martin for me was glamour. I suppose I hoped he might give me a part in a film.'

Andrew looked at her. The admission was made to ease not his wounds but her guilt. It had lost her something in pride, but bought more in confession. 'Never mind,' he said, 'there are plenty more casting couches where that one came from. You'll make it, sweetheart.'

The anger in him as he walked home was, again, not aimed at Lise, particularly. It was cold, not hot.

Among his mail had been bills he'd left for Lise, and junk he'd thrown away. There were two letters to open. One was from his father. The other he opened first: an agent had seen him in the Starters series, and invited him to call on her in Fulham. He threw it away, and opened his father's letter. There was the usual news, and reproach for not having been home for nearly a year, nor written for months. His father sent his greetings to Lise, and remarked how pretty she had looked on television. Knowing that he would soon be a grandfather was splendid news, although he'd have liked to receive it more personally than by courtesy of television. Andrew's mother would have been so glad for him. Not a word about Andrew's comments on his headmaster.

Yes, father, you sired a bastard in me, Andrew said to himself. You never had much luck in anything.

He wrote back at once. He had quit the drama school. Lise had lost her baby, and also they were separated, and intending to divorce. He was sorry to have only bad news to send. He had not written before, waiting for something more cheerful to turn up. But it was best that, for now, the truth be told. His father was not to worry for him, but to look after himself. He would visit when he could, and meanwhile sent his love.

He sealed the envelope, and looked across the kitchen table at Julian and Bad-Feet Willie, drinking coffee. 'I can't bear to meet my father,' he said. 'When I was a kid I loved him, as one does, perhaps more than usually,

112

having no mother. But now . . . We're just two men who once knew each other well. I give him nothing but grief, in pretty well everything I do. He gives me nothing but nostalgia. The pain of knowing. And guilt. That white scarf you wear in bed, Willie – I haven't seen one like it for years. When I was a kid my father bought me one like that, and I was smart and proud in it, with a navy-blue overcoat. And he was so proud of me. I can hardly bear to look at it, that scarf of yours. And yet it's all like a past life, for me. A closed photograph album.'

Willie said, sombrely, 'My father went insane. I think he was jealous of me and my mother.'

'I so much prefer the memory of how my father was,' Andrew went on, 'of how he and I were, that I just can't face seeing him.'

'Why don't you kill him?' Julian asked.

'The memory of how he was?'

'No. Kill him.'

'*I love him.*'

'What you were just saying was that you love the memory of him. You should consider a sacrifice of the present in honour of the past. It's no more than Abraham was prepared to do.'

Andrew stared at Julian, who smiled back, polite and plump, his moustache flexing across his cheeks. His proposition had not been made frivolously, Andrew felt sure.

Too prosaic, the littered betting shop in the afternoon light, to satisfy the metaphysical claims that Julian made for it. His taste in details was fine, Andrew reflected, but he had no sense of theatre. It was roulette, when he discovered it, that was the true cathedral of chance for Andrew. The priest-croupiers, with their fake French imperatives, soon greeted him by name. 'Good evening, Mr Rengard.'

113

'Monsieur Rengard,' he would insist, and often spoke in a marked French accent for the rest of the evening. He bought himself another black suit, of velvet, a frilled black silk shirt, and a floppy black bow-tie, carelessly knotted in front of the mirror every evening at nine, before the black sombrero was added. The whirr and stutter of the ball were as familiar to his ears as his pulse on the pillow, hours later. He seldom sat at the printed baize cloth, preferring to stand where his face was shadowed from the low light. Not that anything could be read in his expression. He trained the muscles of his face, breath, and fingers to be constant wherever the ball fell. The faint arithmetic of those who marked charts he scorned. Every evening he noted the first winning number after his arrival at the table, and bet on the lower adjacent number until 2 pm, increasing his stake when he won. He was proud and polite to every man, courteous to every woman who addressed him.

'Who are you?' he was asked by one of the women who played regularly, after some two weeks.

'Andrew Rengard, ma'am,' he replied, with a slight bow.

She was blonde, not a soft-focus job, but still well made after perhaps ten years of a suburban marriage. 'And who's Andrew Rengard?' she asked.

'I can't tell you that. I could only show you.'

'Show me? How?'

'Rien ne va plus.'

'Excuse me,' Andrew said, and put two chips on number 29. She added one chip of her own. The ball whirred, and stopped in 2.

'Is that showing me?' she asked.

'It could be. It shows me.'

'Shows you who you are, you mean?'

'Certainly.'

'A born loser.'

'You're getting warm.'

'A sucker. Meet another.'

'A born sucker. Yes, that's not far off,' he said, before she could tell him her name.

'Faites vos jeux.'

He put two on 29. She added one. The ball stopped in 35.

'You don't bring me luck,' she said.

'I have none to bring.'

She gave a little smile, and left him. She had had enough. He continued to bet on 29, and it came up twenty minutes later. Her eyes smiled at his across the table, but they did not speak to each other any more.

Julian installed two girlfriends of his in the room Pete and Diana had left. He introduced them as Pinky and Perky, and they had no other names in that house. Pinky worked in a baker's shop, Perky in a sweet factory. Pinky envied Perky's wage-packet, Perky envied Pinky's conditions of work. Neither envied the other her looks. Pinky had a pretty face, framed in dark curls, but her calves were muscular. Perky was justly proud of her long legs, but distressed by her thick, frizzy, ginger hair. 'They're two silly ha'porths,' Julian told Andrew. 'A silly penn'orth. But anyone brighter would upset Willie. He knows these two are just li-los for me.'

Pinky and Perky both adored Sundance, and Emma enjoyed their company, and ready help in the kitchen. Andrew made no attempt to know them, and they thought him a queer fish, though quite dishy, really. So be it.

Julian offered to let one of them, whichever he fancied, share Andrew's bed when he wanted. Andrew thanked him for his kind offer, but declined it. He was migrating through strange realms; that circle of hell was one he did not care to visit.

Julian tricked him, though, one night. It was Willie's birthday (Aries, Virgo in the ascendant), there was a party, and how could Andrew refuse? Julian had left a note for the hashman ordering two extra deals, and there was Pimm's No. 1 for those who preferred it. Andrew promised he would leave the roulette wheel at midnight, and join the party.

When he did, he found only Julian, Willie and the two girls in Willie's room. Emma had been there at the start, but had left to feed Sundance, and not returned. They were surprisingly sober, but greeted him with applause. 'Right,' Julian said, 'everyone have a drink, and now we can get started.' Willie put the first side of *Turandot* on the gramophone, and sat down with a book open in his hand. Julian lined himself and the girls up, with a space left for Andrew, as though for a foursome reel *alla Puccini*. Andrew finished his drink and joined them, in his black velvet suit. Perky, facing him, started to giggle, and infected Pinky. 'Ssssshhh,' Julian cautioned them. 'No larking about. That would spoil it.' Andrew already felt the drink gnaw his gut. It was spiked, he thought. Too late now. Let the wheel spin as it will. The girls had got themselves up to their prettiest, and Willie seemed happy. Andrew was suspicious of what Julian had planned, but could never have guessed.

'There's too many characters in it for me to cast you,' Julian announced, 'so we'll toss a coin for who starts, and from then in take turns at whatever comes up. Call, Andrew.'

'Tails.'

'Tails it is. Right, away you go, Willie.'

And Bad-Feet Willie began to read from what Andrew soon recognised as the start of a chapter in *Fanny Hill*. Perky stepped forward and undressed Andrew of his black clothes, biting her lip in shyness, but with vulnerable eyes, like those of a younger girl reading a teenage paper, discouraging him from stopping her in what she was doing. He saw that Pinky was undressing Julian and he her, and felt obliged to help Perky slip out of her clothes. Then Willie's voice reached the detailed programme of the orgy, and the four of them, to the best of their agilities, performed it through to the end of the chapter. Andrew felt no tenderness for the others, but no disgust, either. It was ludicrous, dreamlike, collective, quite void of intimacy. The girls' naked bodies were extraordinarily more dignified than in their everyday clothes, no matter in what ridiculous couplings and triplings they were joined. Andrew felt a detachment next to holiness upon him, and was amazed. He was sure that Julian had not counted on that, and wondered if he too, nevertheless, was experiencing it.

When Willie finished the reading, Julian handed round more drinks, and proposed a different rite. A man and a woman had between them fifty-six projections and thirteen orifices, allowing in principle seven hundred and twenty-eight varieties of tender penetration. Let them see how many could be achieved simultaneously.

'No, Julian,' Andrew said, 'I'm going to bed. Happy birthday, Bad-Feet Willie.'

Perky slept in his arms that night, and subsequently one of the girls was often waiting in his bed when he returned from the roulette wheel, but it was never anything better than shafting, if that, and the holiness had gone out of it.

An empty church, an empty morning, he is sitting in a pew, resting his forehead on the heels of his hands, and willing his soul to spread its golden wings, to fly up from him. Outside, a bus goes by. In the vestry, a pail clanks on the floor. He kneels. The saints in the windows take no notice of him. He walks to the steps of the altar, and prostrates himself on the dusty red carpet, at the point of

Christ's gaze. 'Jesus,' his hands beseeching the cross, 'scare the shit out of me. Harry me with Thy hounds, until I fall, in a faint, and am devoured. Purify me, O Lord, with that terror I knew once. Quarter my bowels with Thy sword of burning gold.' The expression on Christ's face does not flinch. A heavy lorry passes, another minute.

'Can I help you?'

'Are you the minister?'

'The vicar.' He smiled a tweaky smile, above his dog-collar. 'I heard someone's voice, and came to see if you were all right. You sounded distressed.'

'Of course I did. I was praying.' Andrew was still prostrate on the altar steps, 'Will you join me?'

The vicar looked at his watch, then knelt beside him. 'Our Father,' he began.

'Flail this corrupted earth,' Andrew took over, 'with Thy rods of nuclear fission, so that we may all perish together, effacing all history, all persons, all secret and selfish hopes of salvation. We none of us deserve it, O Lord.'

The vicar had stood up and stepped away, watching him.

'Yes,' Andrew said, 'I am in distress, you see. But don't go and send for the social workers. I know that's what you're thinking. I'm not insane. At least, no more than anyone else. Rather less than most.'

'Are you sure you don't want to be helped?'

'I do want help. I thought you might supply it. Or intercede with Him for me.'

'I can't be your advocate before the Almighty. We all come alone before the seat of judgment. And now, if you'll excuse me.'

'You don't mind if I stay here and keep trying the number?'

'The church is open to everyone, so long as you don't disturb anyone else.'

118

'But that is precisely what I want to do. Timor mortis conturbat me, and I want to pass it on.'

'In that case, I must ask you to finish your prayers, and leave quietly. And please would you sit in one of the pews. This is God's house, and you don't lie on the carpet like that in other people's houses, I take it?'

Andrew stood up, staring darkly at the vicar. The vicar's mouth opened, but he only nodded, and left. Just like the rest of them, Andrew thought, watching him go, an import and export merchant, dealing in bad faith, consigned as pride and dogma.

As he left the church, he saw a notice on the board, that Evensong on the last Sunday in the month would be transmitted on television. It caused him to shut his eyes, and want to weep.

In the roulette room that night, standing beyond the cone of light, he hit a winning streak. The chips stacked up at the edge of the table represented no more than some £60 in that den of modest iniquity, but it was a pretty pile, and attracted the attention of a woman who had once been pretty herself. Drunk, Renata, German, divorced, unlucky, she was, he learned in that order. 'Why don't you come back to my place for a drink?' she asked, and quickly proved that she was no less given to clichés in bed. It is a bad play, Andrew reflected, when she went to sleep. He pocketed a gold cigarette lighter, and left.

Julian was grateful. He offered to pay for the gold, but Andrew, wearing his pendant, did not want the money. 'We need to resuscitate what we have left, here, of the communal spirit. We don't have to mystify our exchanges with money.'

Julian agreed. The house was dispersed in spirit. It was

119

the women's fault. Emma and Sundance were solitary in their room, after meals. Pinky and Perky went out to work, and used the place as a doss-house, albeit they dossed in different beds when the mood was on them. Who needed that? They had not all sat together around the fire since Diana and Pete had left. It was Willie, Julian went on, who gave him anxiety. He spent more time than ever in bed now, complaining about his feet. What would cheer him up, and at the same time restore some shared purpose to the house, would be an act of communal self-assertion.

'What act?' Andrew asked.

'I don't know. But it ought to be something against the outside world, so as to define us as a unit.'

Andrew thought for a while. 'It has also got to express some values we all share, hasn't it?'

Julian pursed his lips beneath his moustache. 'Are there any, do you imagine?'

'There's money. We all scorn it.'

'So how do we express that? Rob a bank?'

'A betting shop might be softer,' Andrew said.

'Liberate a few hundred quid.'

'Well, co-opt it, let's say. And then pile it in the gutter and piss on it.'

'They wouldn't half send us down for that,' Julian said.

'I suppose we could just sprinkle a few oncers of our own and do it. People would still scramble for them.'

'It's not the answer,' Julian said. 'For one thing, it wouldn't cheer Willie up. He's quite warmly attached to money, is Willie. It would upset him.'

'What would please Willie?'

'Let's go and ask him.'

Bad-Feet Willie thought that what was needed was a lament for the last days of civilised society. The beauty has almost gone down behind the horizon, he felt. Mere order is loosed upon the world, and is rationally closing up the enclaves and anomalies in which the imagination used to plant its wild flowers. He pulled his dressing-gown more closely around his shoulders, and gazed gloomily at the foot of his bed.

'So how do we produce that scenario?' Julian asked.

After a while, Willie said, 'We paint our faces white, like sad clowns, with big tears on each cheek, then we dress in city clothes, with bowler hats and brollies, and walk sobbing around the Stock Exchange. Or the Bank of England.'

'It's too passive,' Julian demurred. 'I don't want just to lament the decline of the West. I want to oppose things as they are, throw off our chains and actively have a go at the people who would put them back on us. I'd like to come up with some exemplary act of sacrificing the present to the future.'

'What future?' Willie asked.

'I can't imagine. But it had better be an improvement on what we've got. No, not an improvement, a totally fresh start.'

'By us?' Andrew asked. 'Or by God?'

'It had better be God,' Willie said. 'He'll have more ideas.'

'What God do you worship, then, Willie?' Julian asked.

'The God of Chance.' Willie had played the game before.

'What law do you obey?'

'The Law of Averages.'

'How about this?' Andrew asked. 'We ought to use television in some way, if we want to make the maximum impact. I happened to notice that they're televising a service next week down at that church next to the traffic-lights. It will be going out live, presumably. We ought to find some way of exposing how bloodless the Christian rituals have become.'

Julian was interested. 'If we could get real blood into the communion cup, that would turn a few people on. Or even perform a real sacrifice.'

Andrew interrupted, 'When I said "bloodless" I meant it metaphorically. Their rituals have become empty forms.' Julian was watching him through half-shut eyes, his head held back. Andrew went on, 'What you're suggesting would not be understood.'

'There'd be people who did get the message,' Julian said. 'I'm not out to convert the entire nation. But we couldn't have failed to attract a few apostles.'

'Who or what would you sacrifice?'

'It wouldn't matter, so long as it was in full view of the cameras.'

'What I had in mind,' Andrew said, 'was a satirical gesture, a truly cruel one. For instance, in Sartre's autobiography he tells how his grandfather was a tall, imposing man with a great white beard, and one day, in the local church, very fundamentalist, the priest sang out, "Beware, God is watching you," and at that moment Sartre's grandfather chanced to stride into the church, and there was hysterical panic, they all ran out, terrified. We could stage something on those lines.'

Bad-Feet Willie was giggling, and said he liked it. Julian was shaking his head.

Andrew added, 'He could be carrying a clapperboard to show to the camera, and on it we'd chalk "Creation – Take 2."'

'No,' Julian said. 'You're just talking about acting. I want to talk about action. About power.'

'And glory,' Willie said. 'Don't forget glory.'

'Right,' Julian acknowledged.

'He never does,' Willie assured Andrew, 'never forgets glory.'

'What that lame voluptuary means,' Julian said, 'is that I'm not content to watch myself grow mild and middle-aged and tolerated, and find that I have nothing to show for all my spent energy except a few pendants adorning petit-bourgeois necks. You don't think I'm satisfied to sit at that workbench all my life, do you? If that was the only talent I'd got, I'd have used it to make myself a solid gold hangman's rope. I often think how sweet it would be to twist one of those necklaces around some idiot woman's neck, tighter and tighter. O shut up, Willie, you asked for it.'

Bad-Feet Willie sniffed, and huddled into his dressing-gown. Andrew asked him, 'When he talks about power, he doesn't mean power to the people, I imagine?'

'Bugger the people,' Julian answered. 'They've got it coming. But not your way. Not by little stage-managed satirical gestures, as you call them. That just means a jerk-off, and another postponement. The one certain act that brings the present moment home to everyone is the act of violence. They know that. They've legitimised theirs. We must meet theirs with ours. Nothing else will do. Nothing else will snap the chains we've always been fettered by, and always will be otherwise. An act of violence concentrates the mind wonderfully. On what? On the body. Anyone who witnesses a pure and gratuitous act of violence becomes exhilaratedly aware of his own body. People who watch executions have orgasms, you know. So do the victims. Now, what I'd like us to agree on is to take some institutionalised situation – a church is on the right lines, but it's not the best answer, because it's too old-fashioned and boring for most people to take much notice of – a pop festival might be a better modern equivalent – take that situation, then, and by a simple, direct act reveal the realities, the bodily truths, which underlie it. I've got a picture in my mind which connects with what both of you have suggested, but goes much deeper, I think. David

123

Bowie would be the ideal victim. We don't want a woman. They're unclean, they bleed anyway, periodically. A man's body is intact, proud, beautiful. And we open it. He is Dionysus. He will shriek with suffering and pure joy as we hack him limb from limb. If we take the moment by surprise, no one will dare to stop us until we have completed the ritual. In fact, I hope we'd carry them along with us. It might finish with a true sacrament of blood, I'm not sure. We'd need some others with us, especially to take over the drums. Imagine the rhythm building up. And another thing that I think is desirable is that we're all dressed in various historical costumes, from different periods, to symbolise the collapsing-together and finish, the dead end, of all history in that one intensely bright moment. So that we would be the whole racial memory, and the collective unconscious too, embodied there, to witness the extinction of identity, the authentic sacrifice which welcomes the destiny we all, in our heads, know has got to come. All the wars, and nuclear burn-outs, have just been rehearsals for it, mechanical rehearsals, Armageddonettes.'

Andrew answered, 'One minute you're talking about snapping the chains, the next minute it's the end of history. Aren't you—'

'History is the history of chains.'

'The last time I heard your sermon on this text,' Andrew resumed, 'you said that randomness is the principle we live by, so it would be reasonable, right in fact, that the victims of your violence should be random. I detest that argument. But now you're talking of specifically sacrificing David Bowie.'

'It is the fate he is shaped for. He is quite literally asking for it. He knows his fate. We know ours. But we have this advantage: by welcoming our fate, and promoting it, we can finally release ourselves from its bondage, from randomness. We would have taken history by the neck

124

and strangled it. So we would become the new gods, the deliverers of fate, not its subjects. Mine isn't a static philosophy.'

Andrew looked at Julian, who gazed back into his eyes. On that plump, dark face, now that it had done with its rhetoric, he read the beseechment: Acknowledge that I am I. It was comic. Andrew smiled, his lips rolling back from his teeth, his eyes half-closed. 'Don't you ever read anyone except Nietzsche?'

'If you think I've cooked all this from recipes in books, sweetheart, you shouldn't sit down at the supper table.' Julian outstared Andrew, and left.

After a pause, Bad-Feet Willie remarked, 'On exit lines he is hard to fault, yet.'

'If I thought for a second it was anything more than a game he plays, plays seriously, I'd believe I'd met a perfectly evil man,' Andrew said.

'He's evil, all right.'

'To you?'

'An evil sod to me, very frequently.'

'But it is a game, isn't it? Philosophically, if not in the way he treats you.'

'I'm a practice bout, while he trains for the world title fight.'

'Who with?'

'The world.' Bad-Feet Willie smiled. 'Of course.'

Perhaps he didn't get it from Nietzsche. Perhaps it was cooked up from the brains and guts of the character. Whatever, it was formed under laboratory conditions, a fanatical fiction serving to protect Julian, and probably Willie too, from quotidian doubt. They lived in a sealed compartment, travelling across time. To what station, Andrew speculated, sitting on the back steps in the sunset, what destination, or destiny? None. It could not survive the sceptical bacteria of the air, anywhere.

Sundance was playing in the long, rough grass, crawling from her blanket into the jungle, and rolling back, chuckling, when the lions roared. Emma looked up and smiled to Andrew, shading her eyes against the sunlight reflected from the windows of her room. The windows above, his own, Andrew saw were matt with the city's breath. On the top floor, Bad-Feet Willie's windows were curtained. He smiled back. If his son had been born, Andrew would have wanted him to laugh at lions. Might he, perhaps, have brought him up as a Christian, after all? A Christian who could laugh at lions, like Ferrovius, but would be filled with a proper, chaste terror of eternity, of Christ's suffering, of man's power of will. It was playing evolution false, no doubt, not to bequeath his own loss of faith to his son. But if the alternative were to see his child construct the paltry meanings of the zodiac, or enter the fake eternity of dope, if will dwindled into fate, and dignity into preening like Julian's, then why not? Better that he tell himself a noble lie than a pack of tawdry fibs. As for the truth, it's been remaindered, sorry, sir. Have you tried Socialism? We've had many satisfied customers who've come back for more. Oh sure, I believe it, it did me a lot of good, once. But I was looking for something about myself, not about other people. Or, rather, something about my son, here. Sundance was sucking her thumb, on Emma's shoulder. Andrew was remembering a remark of Martin's, 'Democracy is a trade-union of the small-minded.' Emma was closing her eyes, in the sunlight.

'It's a beautiful time, isn't it?' she said, shutting the book she had been reading.

Andrew nodded. 'I expect so.'

'Can't you feel it?'

'No. I'm like my windows up there. Look. So grimy with being in this city that almost nothing can filter through any more. So all I can do is imagine, or remember, what it must feel like to you, to sit in the sun, with Sundance, and just be spontaneous.'

'Why don't you clean them?'

'My windows, you mean? Or myself?'

'Both.'

'I'd have to be an optimist. I haven't got the energy.' Lise has taken it all away, he thought, all my hope. I was a son, then a lover, and both times a loser. They never come back.

Sundance was playing a new game, in Emma's arms, letting herself fall back from the waist, until her mother's hand caught her head. 'Careful,' Andrew said. 'That looks dangerous for her. She could rick her back, or something.'

Emma, the effort of coping with Sundance on her face, shook her head. 'She's like rubber. It's what we all want to be like again, when we're into yoga, and that kind of thing. Look.' She laid the baby down on its back, and folded the podgy little legs around the back of its head. Sundance gurgled. Emma smiled down at her baby.

'She looks very well,' Andrew said.

'She's fine. I took her to the clinic last month and they were delighted with her.' Emma picked the baby up, and cuddled her. 'There was a bit of worry about me, actually, because I'd got some sort of lump here on my breast, and it's after you've weaned a baby that you can develop breast cancer, you know? Especially when you have your first baby when you're in your late twenties.'

'I didn't know that,' Andrew said. 'No.'

'Well, they say so, anyway. But it's all right, it's nothing much after all, just a cyst. I heard from them about it last week, and I've never loved the sunshine so much in all my life. Do you think that sounds silly?'

'No,' Andrew said gravely. 'You're a lucky woman. I envy you.'

'Oh, don't envy me. I'd hate to be envied by anyone. Be glad of what you are.'

And he did try, believe me. He sat in his room, hunting through his heart for blessings he could count. He thought how nice it would be if he and Emma were in love, and lived together, with Sundance, and more babies. Nice was the word, he knew it: nice, sweet, boring. She had no pit in her, no brimstone, black laughter, none of the irony in the soul that makes us distinctively human. She was a natural child of nature, and would die one. Probably there are many like her in the world, doing no harm, ever. All the music they need is folk songs. None of the orchestral faith-healers, like this Elgar, putting back what the living took out. As he walked to the roulette table through the night, he sang to himself from Bad-Feet Willie's *Turandot*,

O amante smunta dei morti!

He was a black cipher in the black light, and abandoned himself fiercely to the wheel. Renata came to stand beside him, and asked him if he had seen a gold lighter of hers, that she had mislaid.

'Yes. I took it.'

'Took it? Where to?'

'I gave it away, to a friend.'

'You bastard,' she said, in a tone of acclamation.

He lost at roulette, and the fierceness was still on him, a fierce pride in himself, when he got home, and, finding neither Pinky nor Perky waiting for him, went into their room, and their shared bed, like a lion, a dying, raging lion.

'More like a wolf,' Pinky giggled, when he lifted his dark Celtic face, and snarled.

'Ay,' he said, 'a wolf in black sheep's clothing.'

'Very clever,' Perky said. 'What a shame you're not an actor.'

'I'm an impostor. What's the difference?'

'Search me.'

'I will.'

Afterwards, he lay a long time awake, eyes unclosed, in the little death, suffering the natural reflex of the primitive nervous system, the reciprocal recoil toward disintegration after the most intense pursuit of life, rehearsing the evolutionary pattern. The girls, asleep beside him, they are simple girls, he thought, silly perhaps, but with a generosity of instinct that few clever girls have. They don't barter their bodies, they share them, and expect no return on their capital except to enjoy another shared body. It's when people suppress their sexuality, to give it a rare exchange value, like gold, that they put in the heads of men like me the appetite for exciting adventures on the tiger skin. Men like me and Martin. Mon semblable! I hate him for that, more than anything else.

And yet, there was that negative capability that Lise had gone on about, and perhaps it took that form, infallibly, a protean adaptation to match any subject. The chameleon of the camera. A creature that stalks its prey by mimicry, then snaps in, sucking the juice, sapping the veins and heart, the ideas out of the brain, till the husk falls from its mouth. Like an actor's predatory fall upon his character. Or a writer's. Yet Lise had not allowed herself to be sucked dry. At what cost, that visit from Sybil. Why, Andrew mused, had it not been himself that Sybil attacked, for permitting it to happen between the other pair?

He closed his eyes, and wanted to see Lise, just once more. He was no good without her. She had filleted him. He started to compose what he could say to her, be for her. To plead, to appeal, would irresistibly tempt her scorn. You always kill the love you won. He would go to her pale, cool, ruthless, proud, polite, to let her see what she had passed up; be so glassy that he would reflect back to her the sense of herself divided by ironies.

'We've decided we like your idea about the church when the television people are there,' Julian said. He was stripped to the waist, sitting against the wall in Bad-Feet Willie's room. Willie was lying full length on the floor, smiling. Julian offered Andrew a smoke. 'It's good Moroccan, only just come in.'

Andrew sat on the floor and joined in. 'I thought you preferred the persecution and assassination of David Bowie?'

'Willie's not bowled over by that idea, are you, Willie boy?' Julian leaned over to tickle Willie's neck.

Willie giggled. 'I like his singing, that's my objection. Someone drearier would take his place.'

'So,' Julian went on, 'we've figured out a scenario for the church next Sunday. All we need is quite a small megaphone.'

'The worst they could do us for,' Willie said, 'is a breach of the peace that passeth all understanding.'

'What exactly do we do?' Andrew asked.

'Just let them hear the word of the Lord,' Julian answered, 'the word of the Lord.' And he collapsed, laughing, upon Willie. Looking up at Andrew, he added, 'You've been cast as the Lord, by the way. You've done the research. We'll do the rest.'

'And the girls?'

'We don't need them.'

The skin on Lise's face is like a petal about to fall. What was sheen is texture now, mortal, coloured, and there are two spots on her chin. It makes it easier.

130

'I suppose you'd better come in,' she said.

Andrew stepped into the hall. 'Have you got someone here?'

'No. Why?'

'You seemed reluctant to ask me in.'

'I am. I'm not sure I should ever shut a door behind us, from the divorce point of view, apart from anything else.'

'What else?'

She gave him a faint, sardonic smile, and led him into the sitting-room. 'You might as well have a drink, now you're here. Gin all right?'

Andrew nodded. 'The divorce coming along okay?'

'Yes. You're not surprised?'

'No. What grounds?'

'It's not a question of grounds any more. You just have to show it has all broken down irretrievably. That shouldn't overtax my solicitor.'

'Your brother Ben?'

'No. Someone he recommended. He couldn't act for me.'

'Ben couldn't act for a million pounds.'

'You haven't come here just to make smart remarks about my family.' Her eyes, her sweet eyes, they are saying nothing but Got and Want.

'How about your acting?' Andrew asked. 'Did anything come of that television introduction Martin got for you?'

'I've seen the producer. He thinks he can get me something after I've finished here.'

'When is that? I've lost track.'

'The end of next month.'

'So you're working on the end-of-year show now?'

'Yes. Christ, you look awful, do you know, Andrew?'

'Yes. I've been indulging myself in every luxury, except remorse.'

'Lucky old you.'

'How about you?'

131

'I had a holiday, on Ibiza.'

'With your family?'

'No, I went on my own, as a matter of fact.'

'And stayed on your own?'

'Yes.'

'You're lying.'

She looked at him. 'All right, why should I bother to tell stories to you? You aren't cross-petitioning. Martin was there for precisely thirty-six hours.

'Now you're telling the truth, and it tastes bitter.'

'No, not bitter at all. It was very sweet, while it lasted. It wasn't his fault he couldn't stay longer. He had to get back to Jugoslavia.'

'And to Sybil.'

'That's right, back to Sybil.'

'It's the eternal tripod.'

'Is this what you've come here for, in your smart black suit?'

'I'm finishing my drink. So you've forgiven him for driving Sybil round here?'

Lise shrugged, and looked out of the window. 'He had no alternative.'

'He had no choice, you mean.' Her fingers around the glass looked like old friends to Andrew. He admired how she was keeping them relaxed. She had worked hard at the school, this year. But she is being eaten alive by the bitch Ambition, to be an actress. The old story. So be it.

'I'll tell you something you'll enjoy,' Lise said. 'She has a private detective tailing him.'

'Yes, I did enjoy that. Otherwise, how was Ibiza?'

'Fantastic. Just like the Martini ads. It made me want to forget all about the theatre, and just go and live in the sun, with some people I met out there. They're completely self-sufficient, you know. They grow all they need. The trouble is, even Ibiza isn't going to last much longer. They're building new roads all over the place, and sticking up electricity lines, and things.'

'Nice for the Ibizencos, though.'

'No. They'll know what they've lost, soon enough.'

It is as though she has an icy core of hysterical fear within her, and it is irradiating her, like cobalt, and destroying that fine flesh. To be honest, it is a great relief. Even to imagine being able to do without her.

'Well,' she said, putting her glass down, 'if there really is nothing you've come to say . . .'

'I'll just have another drink, thanks.' He poured himself one, and offered her the bottle, but she ignored it. 'How are your parents?'

'They're in great form, thankyou. I'm going down to spend next week with them in Dorset. My father has got a fortnight off, and I've got a week I can spend learning lines. I'll tell them you made a point of coming round to ask after them.'

'Do, please. Cheers.' He was glittering black glass. 'That's nice,' he said, picking up a gold double-bangle. He put it in his pocket, and drank down the gin.

'That's not yours,' Lise said.

'No. I'm just taking it.'

'It's my property.'

'Property is theft.'

'So theft is property.'

'I'm not going to keep it. I'm taking it for a friend.'

'Maid Marian, would that be?'

'A feller, actually. A goldsmith. He made this pendant for me. Do you like it? No, I'm not into redistribution from the rich to the poor. It's all wholly spontaneous. Random, in fact. The only true Socialist is a jackdaw.'

'Are you going to give it back to me?'

'No. Thanks for the drink. Give Martin my love, next time you see him. Is he any better in bed now, incidentally?'

'I'm not complaining.'

'He must have been practising with someone.'

They have come to this, then, to believing in the man in the Martini ad. It is all they have left. We have disappointed them in every last way. The fate of women in England now!

Andrew let himself out. There would be a threatening letter from her solicitor about the bangle, but she wouldn't know where to post it to.

'Oh Lord, have mercy upon us miserable sinners,' the congregation begged.

'No way,' the stone walls whispered back, immediately.

Not one of the bowed heads in the packed church lifted or breathed. The vicar was frozen open-mouthed. It must be something to do with the television. They might have told him.

Andrew was kneeling low down in the pew, with the megaphone angled to the stone floor. Close on each side of him Julian and Bad-Feet Willie were sitting forward so that their coats masked him. Their eyes met in gratification. The effect was better than they had hoped, an echo insinuating itself throughout the church and the pious network, yet, to judge by the whispers and peering now going on, impossible to locate at source. Julian gave Andrew a nod, and the Litany ended,

'O Lord, deal not with us after our sins.'

'Neither reward us after our iniquities.'

'Repent, you hypocrites, do you hear? Repent, already.'

As they stood, Andrew was jabbed violently in the kidneys. An elderly woman in the pew behind had rumbled them, and now went on stabbing him with her umbrella, staring wildly through steel-rimmed spectacles. He tried to hold her umbrella, but she was strong in her rage, chattering, and hit him in the face with the handle. Others around them realised what was going on, and saw the megaphone inside Andrew's coat. A sidesman hurried down the nave toward the incident. The organ was striking up, *Guide Us, O Thou Great Redeemer*. Julian led the way out of the pew, erect and impassive, in spite of the hymn-books, prayer-books, umbrellas and sticks that were hitting them. Andrew followed, along the nave, through the door, and down the steps.

'Where's Willie?' Julian asked, abruptly.

Andrew turned to look. Framed in the doorway were three furious worshippers, including the sidesman, debating whether to give chase. 'I assumed he was following me,' Andrew said.

'O Jesu,' Julian said, 'with his feet you know he couldn't dodge them. You were supposed to fucking help him.' Julian ran back up the steps, and plunged through the crowded doorway. The people there turned their backs to Andrew. He decided not to follow, but waited. After a minute, Bad-Feet Willie came out of the door, held by two men. Julian, behind him, was also held. He had a cut eyebrow, and blood around his eye.

While Andrew stood watching, two policemen ran past him, and up the steps. The sidesman pointed at Andrew, and one of the policeman ran back down, and arrested him.

When the vicar arrived at the police station, he insisted that he did not want them to be charged. 'Fortunately,' he said, 'the television producer assures me that almost nothing of the incident will have been seen by people watching the broadcast, and in the circumstances I'd rather not give people like this the publicity which is what they do it for. It would be a good story, as they say, for the press, when it came up in court. I don't want to give them that satisfaction.'

The duty sergeant was frowning, and shaking his head. 'You've got to teach them, vicar. They'll only do it again next week, if you don't.'

135

Andrew formed his index fingers into a cross, and held them out toward the vicar's face. 'The Church Militant of Emmanuel the Visionary will be triumphant when the last trump sounds,' he intoned, staring madly.

'Emmanuel! Emmanuel!' Julian and Willie shouted, and started to dance.

The sergeant put his hand over his eyes, and shook his head again.

'Your old men shall dream dreams,' Andrew went on, 'and your young men shall see visions. The Book of Joel, two, twenty-eight.'

'That right?' the sergeant asked the vicar. The vicar nodded.

'Hallelujah!' Julian and Willie agreed. 'Hallelujah!'

'But man has closed himself up,' Andrew went on, 'till he sees all through narrow chinks of his own cavern, saith the holy William.'

'Hallelujah!'

One of the constables who had arrested them came to stand directly in front of Andrew. He was the same height, and age, and his face was also dark in the Celtic mould. They stood there, eye to eye, both sneering, prevented from changing places only by the uniform on one, the pendant on the other. 'You on drugs?' the constable enquired.

Andrew threw his head back, and bellowed to the ceiling, 'Our prophet hath said, "The Lord hath given thee fruit of the trees, roots of the ground, yea, and clear waters of the spring. Wherefore then seek ye other sustenance?" '

'LSD, is it? Empty out your pockets.'

But their pockets were innocent, and only their names and address were kept at the station.

On the pavement outside, the vicar said to Andrew, 'I remember you from the other morning. Look, I respect your beliefs, whatever they might be. All I ask is that you respect mine, and my congregation's.'

136

'Hallelujah!' Julian whooped, and spat in the vicar's face.

'There was no need,' Andrew said, in Willie's room.

'Exactly so,' Julian answered.

'That is why it was beautiful,' Willie went on, 'an un-necessary evil. If you waste your talents on just doing the things you need to do, you grow old with it. You foreclose all your options. Julian has a beautiful soul because he re-invents himself every morning. Am I talking too slowly, do you think?'

'Have you read Tolstoy's *Resurrection*?' Andrew asked.

'I expect so,' Julian said. 'What shall we do tomorrow?'

'Who do you want to be?' Willie asked.

'Listen,' Andrew said, 'let's just clear up this one point about today, first.'

'Clear up my arse,' Julian said quietly. 'You've got a mind like a hoover gone berserk.'

'It sucked us out of the mess in the drum, didn't it?'

'Having first decanted us into it by abandoning Willie. It was the very least we could expect of you. Don't forget the scenario was your idea, in the first place, and frankly it turned out to be pitiful. A temporary fault in the suburban rituals of the petit-bourgeoisie, that's the extent to which we burst the chains of injustice. The State is not quite on its last legs, yet, wouldn't you concede? A request that the last one to leave the country should switch the lights off, please, would be premature.'

'I could justify what we did,' Andrew answered, in a voice of black glass. 'Of course I could. I am one of the great justifiers. I could justify the iceberg to the Titanic. When I am in the justifying vein, Jesuits go pale.'

'I believe you,' Julian said. 'It's the same talent as the one which goes around looking for outstanding points to clear up. You're the daily help of the revolution.'

137

'What we did,' Andrew continued calmly, 'was to puncture one lie. A very tiny lie, I admit. But it was more than we achieve by sitting in a room, smoking pot. And in the days when I used to believe that all the lies could be punctured, that would have been my justification. Now, in fact, I don't believe that any more. We can't puncture them all. We don't need to, even. Gradually, they're puncturing themselves, wearing through, rubbing on their own contradictions. When I remember I'm an Anarchist, I'm glad about that. On all sides, governments of all tendencies are collapsing. But the transition is going to be more murderous yet. There are so many lies that need to enact themselves until they're exhausted, or worn through. Meanwhile, it seems to me that sitting quietly in a room is the duty one owes oneself. What we did today I understood we did only to enrich the communal sense we have, or should have, in this house. You it was who restricted it to just the three of us, but that's by the way. But now you're talking about the revolution, and the injustice of the State. That is a different game of marbles, and I'm out of practice. I've been assuming that our immediate objective is to hollow out a private sanctuary within the conditions imposed by the State. What you want, it seems from what you said, is to explode the whole cheese.'

Bad-Feet Willie clapped. Andrew bowed. 'Not bad, I confess, after all this time away from the boards.'

Julian's face had altered. He spoke thoughtfully. 'You're right. We've got to keep politics out of revolution. Our responsibility is absolutely personal. You've understood that. But your error is forgetting that our only path to true freedom is to release cosmic energy, which means to split the nucleus in which we and the social order have been bonded together. That is why we must create an act of violence against the social order as it presents itself to *us*. We are not required to analyse the general, objective situation which everyone else shares with us. But we cannot sit quietly in this room, and be free, and love each other, until we have blown the oppressive father-figures out of our own heads.'

Willie was gazing at Julian's face, and nodding agreement. Hallelujah! Andrew was tired of words, words, his own as much as other people's. Words were like money: you scribble amounts and signatures on bits of paper, and you land in shtuck when you get the scribbling wrong. No one comes and tells you to work harder, they just confront you with their own incontestable scribbles. He scarcely followed Julian's argument. The assurance in the voice was seductive as vertigo to his mourning soul.

'Today,' Julian was saying, 'there was no father-figure, merely a puny little priest. It followed that our action could be no more than a satirical hiccough, a feeble gesture on behalf of an alternative society. There is no alternative society. To co-exist is to be beleaguered. If you take no notice of them, they will certainly take notice of you. We must act against them. We must, before it is too late. Do you agree?'

'Any course of action will suit me,' Andrew answered, 'just so long as I don't have to believe in it.'

He was used to it, being watched by faces footlighted in the reflection off the green baize table, where he stood, outside the cone, dark, elegant, hieratic, unwinking, but the man with Renata tonight was evidently casing his joints.

The wheel spun. For months, now, it had entered his dreams every night, and by day he could not see a car halt, or a ferris wheel, a gramophone record play, without a silent wager on where the ball would land. All this evening he had lost. It was his last chip on 34, the wheel spun, and he murmured, 'Baby wants new shoes.' The ball skipped, and came to rest in 25. Andrew turned and left the room, as usual, but outside the door, in the lobby, he stood against the wall, and waited. Before the door had stopped swinging, the man came out with Renata.

Andrew looked him steadily in the eyes. The man looked at Renata, then said to Andrew, 'Can I have a word with you?'

'Sure.'

'Outside.'

'Here will do.'

'No it won't.'

Andrew shrugged, and walked back into the roulette room. He bought a fresh stack, and started to play 34 again.

The man came to stand beside him, and murmured, 'What sort of bastard are you, then? A coward, too?'

'You'll find me in the Yellow Pages under Manic-Depressives.'

'Are you going to give her that gold lighter back?'

'I can't. It's been melted down.'

'A hundred and fifty quid, then.'

Andrew staked on 34 again.

'Or you'll be coming here on wheels in future.' The man gestured below the level of the table.

Andrew cocked his eye, and eyed his cock. He picked up another chip, and showed it to the man. 'Look, mon ami,' he said, 'that is what I value my life at.' He added it to the other chip. The wheel spun, and a woman who had staked on 2-3-5-6 sighed as she won. 'It's gone,' Andrew said. 'My life belongs to me no more. It was a gambling debt. Take it.' He handed the man a chip, and nodded at the table. The man looked at him, and staked the chip on 20. The ball came to rest in 17.

'I am not here to play games with you,' the man whispered. 'I am here to collect a hundred and fifty pounds from you. If you haven't got it with you, we are going to your place, and if you haven't got it there we are waiting until you do get it.'

140

'I am a martyr to other people's confidence in me,' Andrew said. 'Where should I get such money?'

'You must have got something for that lighter.'

'I gave it away, in payment of another debt, of a kind. I have nothing worth a hundred and fifty pounds. Did you know that the son of a French executioner once ran up severe gambling debts, and in order to pay them off he pawned his father's guillotine?' Andrew laughed out loud.

The man whispered, 'You won't be laughing much longer.'

The woman who had won on 2-3-5-6 had lost it all again, and stood up, saying, 'It's not fair.'

'Of course it's not fair,' Andrew told her. 'What do you want, a jury?'

The man said, 'For someone who is going to be crippled for life, you are very cool.'

Andrew staked on 34 again. 'I'm just papering over the wisecracks.'

The wheel paid on 34 that spin. As the thirty-six chips were pushed toward him, Andrew said, 'If I put all of these on red, and it comes up twice running, you've got your money. If it loses, we forget about it all, right?'

'No. I am here to collect, not to gamble.'

Taking no notice, Andrew staked the stack on red. The wheel spun, and it was red. He left the doubled stack in place. Again, red won.

'That was the luckiest win of your life,' the man whispered. 'You wouldn't have had a life worth speaking of, if you hadn't won.'

Andrew stood where he was. The stack remained on red. The wheel paid on black. 'So it goes,' Andrew murmured.

The man held his jacket open, in front of Andrew, and let him see a switch-blade flash open. He stared into Andrew's eyes. 'I am not playing silly buggers,' he said.

'I could see that with half an eye. Though whether half

an eye is better than no bread will continue to be debated, I expect.'

'Are you ready?' the man asked, putting his knife away.

'Ready?'

'To go to your place.'

'I've got nothing there.'

'We'll see.'

Andrew cashed in his chips. The man walked him out of the club, his shoulder touching the back of Andrew's. Renata followed. 'Get in,' the man said, when they reached a blue Volvo. Andrew got in the back, Renata in the front passenger seat. 'Watch him,' the man told her, gunning the engine, 'to see he don't knock me on the head. Don't try jumping out the door,' he added to Andrew. 'They won't open from the inside. Child-proof, you see.'

Andrew gave him a false address, and waited for traffic-lights to come up red. When they did, his foot was ready on the release catch in front of him, beside the driving seat. He pressed it down, and the driver, as he braked, slid forward on to the steering wheel. Andrew took his right foot from the catch, and kept the man pinned by thrusting against the seat with his left leg. He wound down the rear window, and reached through it to open the door. The engine was shrieking, because the driver's foot was flat down on the accelerator, trying to lever the seat back against Andrew's straight leg. Renata was scrabbling over her seat at Andrew, but he had a hand free to fend her off, and once the door was open he rolled out of the car, tearing himself clear of the fingerholds she had on his jacket, abandoning his sombrero to her. He ran back along the road to the corner of a sidestreet. There, he glanced toward the traffic-lights. The man was just pulling away, straight on, settling for next time and no mistake.

The car Julian hired the next day was a white

142

Volkswagen, and again Andrew sat in the rear seat, directing them through Dorset lanes. It was a clear, sunny day, in the middle of May. The road shimmered, inverting trees, the sea sparkled in distant glimpses. They stopped for twenty minutes, to watch a village cricket match, drink whiskey, and check through their game plan. They drove on, until Andrew told Julian to turn along a cart-track, between hedges, and leave the car behind a derelict stone-built hut, out of sight of the road.

Julian put on a peaked cap large enough to shade his eyes. He got out of the car to put on a heavy, navy-blue raincoat, and pulled the collar up around his jowls. From under the driving seat he took out a double-barrelled shotgun. He showed Andrew the cartridges before he loaded them. 'Blanks. Okay?' Andrew nodded. Julian concealed the gun beneath his coat, and held it there with his right hand. In his left he picked up a clipboard, with some papers on it. Willie took hold of a grip on the rear seat. Julian looked at the other two, and said, 'Let's go.'

They followed a sheeptrack that curved on the contour of a hill. The house came into sight, three hundred yards on round the hillside, slightly below where they now stood. It was a two-storey thatched farmhouse, with white-plastered cob walls. Rhododendrons screened the west side that faced them. At the far end of the rhododendrons was a brick garage, from which a gravel drive led out past the south front of the house and around the farther side of the hill, between elms, oaks, and shrubs. At the back of the house, the hill came sharply down to meet it. On its farther side, and in front, were roughly-mown lawns, sloping away. Nobody was in sight.

Julian nodded, and went on ahead, scratching his left brow so that his clipboard masked his face from anyone who might look out from the window above the rhododendrons. When he reached the blind rear wall of the garage he peered around it, and beckoned. While the

143

other two followed, Julian kept watch on the window.

Behind the garage, Willie opened the grip and each of them took a pink rubber half-mask, with a pig's snout and piggy eyeholes, and pulled it on. Willie added a judge's wig to his mask, so did Andrew. Julian replaced his cap, concealed the gun again, and walked up to the front door of the house, bending his head as if consulting the clipboard. He knocked on the door. Lise, in jeans and a shirt, opened it. Julian brought the gun out, and levelled it at her. Willie and Andrew joined them.

Lise did not speak, or move. 'Turn round,' Julian told her, and she did. Julian took the cap off and handed it to Willie, who exchanged it for another wig. Julian shouted 'Help!' There was no answer. 'Where are the others?' he asked.

'They're not here,' Lise replied.

'Where are they?'

'They've gone home.'

'How long for?'

'I don't know.'

Julian prodded the gun into her back. 'How long for?'

'Really, I don't know. They weren't sure. Tomorrow, some time.'

'Walk slowly through that door on the left.'

Lise obeyed. Julian and Willie followed her in. Andrew shut the front door and bolted it, ripped out the telephone cable in the hall, and joined the others in the drawing-room. It was as he remembered it, and he was faint with nostalgia. The chesterfield where Lise now sat, and the armchairs, loose-covered with a pretty Heal's fabric, aquamarine with white camellias; the walls painted white, with framed equestrian prints, and a big oil-painting, a garden by David Inshaw, on the wall facing the door; the plank floor sanded, and painted with clear polyurethane, covered in the centre of the room by a large, dark-blue and green carpet; beneath the Inshaw, an

144

escritoire; facing it, next to the door, an open fireplace, with inglenooks; along the wall facing the windows, through which the sun shone warmly, a low, long bookcase, filled with uniform sets of Dickens, Shakespeare, George Eliot, Thackeray, Trollope, Jane Austen, lines of Penguins, a corner of paperback thrillers, some books on travel, cookery, painting, biographies; above the bookcase a gilt-framed Georgian mirror; here and there silver ornaments, some porcelain figures, an occasional table, magazines littered on its glass top and shelf, *Punch*, *The Lady, New Statesman, Country Life, Private Eye, Nova*, and several copies of the parish magazine.

'Why didn't you go with them?' Julian was asking Lise.

'I wanted to stay here. I've got some work I have to do.'

'You could have done it at home.'

'I like it here. It's peaceful. Or was. What do you want? There's no money, to speak of. I've got a few pounds in my bag, that's all. The silver would easily be traced. I think you're wasting your time, really.'

Julian said nothing.

'The same with that painting,' Lise went on, 'they'd easily trace that. We don't keep anything of much value down here, can't you see that? It's a country—'

'Shut up.' Julian jerked his head to tell Willie and Andrew to leave the room. 'Don't move,' he told Lise.

They stood in the hall, watching her through the open door. 'Is she telling the truth,' Julian asked quietly, 'about her parents being away for the night?'

'It figures,' Andrew murmured. 'Probably some legal dinner he has to go to, in town. It is Whit weekend, isn't it?'

'Damn,' Julian said. 'We'll have to guard her all night, till they come.' Andrew and Willie nodded. 'We should have thought of telephoning first to check them all out,' Julian went on. 'Well, we might as well try her for now. It will be a rehearsal for the big one.'

145

They went back into the drawing-room. 'Get that little table out of the way,' Julian said. Andrew and Willie carried it to the wall, then, directed by Julian, brought the escritoire in front of the fireplace, with a chair behind it, facing across the room. Two other upright chairs were brought in, and set one each side of the escritoire chair.

Julian commanded Lise, 'Lie down on the carpet, face down.' She did so. The three bewigged pigs went out of the door. Julian and Andrew entered again, and sat in the flanking chairs. When Willie entered, they stood up. 'Silence in court,' Julian barked. Willie took his seat in the central chair, the other two sat down again, and Julian once more arose.

'M'luds,' he began, 'the case you are to try today relates, as your lordships will know, to the notorious gang of father-figures who have for many centuries terrorised this land, masquerading under the gang-title of Society.'

The judge in the middle honked twice. 'Continue,' he said.

'This wretched creature who prostrates herself before you today is, in herself, quite plainly no father-figure. Did she but know it, she is no less a victim of that Society—'

Honk-honk, went Bad-Feet Willie.

'—of that Society by which we are required to suppress our desires and satisfactions, in a word, our freedom. But she does not know it, m'luds, not yet, and it is my earnest hope that this court will assist her to that knowledge by the judgments that it will hand down in cases later in these sessions. At that juncture, I shall not be inviting your lordships to hear the argument that each and every tyrant in our brains must be destroyed. Possibly that is so. But it may prove that just one will be sufficient. We shall see. Because they are a linked chain, m'luds, like cut-out paper dolls. They surround us with their illusion of three-dimensionality, but only one dimension links them, and that, m'luds, is their encircling enmity to our freedom.

Therefore we, who oppose what that Society calls its order, we must act against them on that same dimension. We must destroy one of the respectable monsters, in order to tear their illusory links apart, and see them for what they are. And should one not suffice, then others must be arraigned before your lordships, and duly sentenced, until the chains are snapped.'

Honk, went Willie. 'An elegant argument, Mr Swinefever.'

'Thank you, m'lud. If we do not act against them thus, we must suffer. If we suffer, we are not free, our destiny cannot play itself out till the end of time. Instead of by fate, we will be bound by regulations. Instead of chance, we will accept order. Their order. For they will always hate our freedom, our authenticity, just as Satan hates the cross.

'I thank your lordships for your indulgence during that digression. It was necessary for the court to be acquainted with the background before which this pitiable woman has been living in bad faith. In a woman, your lordships will I am sure concur, bad breath is regrettable, bad faith unpardonable. Her crime, m'luds, is more easily described than forgiven. She has lived in the house of one of the most noted tyrants of all—'

Honk-honk-*honk*.

'—yes, and been succoured by him all her days, without once having raised her voice to question him, still less assail him, with regard to the heavy ego-trip he enjoys every day at the expense of those comrades of ours who have seen the light, as well as the dark. She is, m'luds, a collaborator, a fellow-traveller, in first-class. Before she enters her defence, I would ask your lordships to beware of her honeyed speech. Fine words, as several people have noted, are of limited application when there are parsnips to be buttered. Indeed, the sceptical men of Yorkshire maintain, I understand, that they are no use at all.'

Julian sat down.

'Have you anything to say before we reach our verdict, and pass sentence?' Bad-Feet Willie asked.

Lise lay still on the floor.

'Speak!' Julian commanded.

Lise shook her pretty head.

'Oh come,' Julian reproached her. 'You have allowed yourself to exist in a forest of ambiguities for years. The ambiguity of body against head, or of instinct against father, to name but a couple of the trees. These are the ambiguities which prevent the true revolutionary spirit – and I do not speak only of a left-wing revolution – which prevent that spirit from committing itself to what it most wants, passionately wants to give birth to. Now the game is up, my girl, and it is time for you at least to confess to your crime, even if no phrases of mitigation follow. You must have something to say?'

Lise said, 'I can't find the words to say what I'm feeling.'

'Feeling?' Julian answered. 'What have your feelings got to do with politics? Tell the truth, young lady, that is my advice to you.'

Lise lay silent.

'M'luds?' Julian addressed his fellow judges.

Andrew, in a guttural voice, said, 'Corsned.'

'Corsned,' Julian repeated. 'My lordship has pronounced a verdict to which I know he is very partial. As he has explained it to me, it is an ancient ordeal in which the accused is forcibly fed on consecrated bread and cheese. If she chokes, she is guilty. An admirable verdict, m'lud.' Julian clapped, and Willie joined in. Andrew rose, and bowed, then all three danced around Lise, their wigs flapping their pig-faces, whooping and yippeeing.

Julian signalled the others to be seated again, and said, 'An excellent verdict, m'luds, but may I beg the court's patience in administering it. I propose that it take place tomorrow, when greater villains than this wretched girl will be before the court, and may learn from the example that she will give them, in her ordeal. Meanwhile, may it please your lordships that, to assure ourselves that the accused be not tempted to escape from this place, she be required to undress herself?'

'Agreed,' Willie honked. 'Court adjourned.'

Lise lay still, and nobody spoke, until Julian curtly told her, 'Go on then, strip.' He poked her in the back with his gun.

'Here?' Lise asked, still face to the carpet.

'Yes.'

She stood up, and took her clothes off, not looking at the others, but with hatred in her eyes, and her jaw. When she had only her white panties left on she hesitated. Julian answered by reaching forward with the gun, and pulling the top of the panties down with it. She took them off, and sat in an armchair, her arms along her thighs, hands clasped, looking down at her feet.

They found some ham and cheese to eat, claret and cognac to drink, played records of Bach, Elgar, Ravel, the Stones and the Beatles, and all the time Lise moved hardly at all, except to take some food and a glass of wine. At sunset, Julian went out for a stroll, and shortly Lise asked if she might put some clothes on, because she was cold.

'I don't think you ought to put those clothes back on,' Willie said. 'The idea is, you won't be tempted to try and run off.'

'A blanket, then?'

Willie looked at Andrew. Andrew nodded. Willie, who was holding the gun, said, 'Could you go and get one? My feet, you know.'

'Wait,' Lise said, 'I'd better go and get it myself. I know where they are.'

'Hold it there,' Willie said, jumping up and pointing the gun.

'He can come with me as a guard, can't he?' Lise asked.

149

Willie looked at Andrew again. Andrew nodded, and opened the door. He followed Lise upstairs, and waited on the landing. She came out of a bedroom with a blanket around her, and whispered to him, 'How have you got mixed up with clowns like that?'

Andrew was dumbfounded.

'Oh, of course I know it's you,' Lise went on. 'You don't seriously think you could walk across a room, or sit down in a chair, without my recognising you, do you?'

'I thought I was doing a fair job of acting a part different from myself,' Andrew whispered.

Lise smiled, and walked downstairs, back into the drawing-room. Andrew went for a pee. When he shook himself, a few drops scattered on the white drill trousers that Julian had lent him. The small humiliations of the bathroom, he thought. Especially the de Witts' bathroom.

Now that Lise had fingered him, he could not imagine the outcome. She had been clever to get him alone; but if she really had it in for him she would not have let on at all. He was glad, anyway, that she had something to wrap round her body. He had hated it that Julian and Willie could see Lise naked. 'You can take your own revenge any time you like,' Julian had said to him in the kitchen.

Julian arranged the night watches. Each guard would have two hours' sleep in turn, leaving two to stay with Lise. Andrew said he was not at all tired, and preferred to sit up, so Willie was first to sleep, then Julian.

At 4.30 that Pentecostal morning, Willie started to snore. Andrew looked at him, in an armchair, the gun resting across the arms of it. Between them, they had drunk three bottles of claret, and nearly two of cognac. Willie was not going to wake up easily. No Cerberus he. Julian was on a bed upstairs. Andrew looked at Lise, lying on the chesterfield. She was watching him. Probably she had not slept at all. Her face was tired. The bitch Ambition had left it. She looked as she had often looked, to Andrew, waking in the early morning. 'O God,' he said. 'Lise.'

She held her arms open to him, lifted his mask, and took his face between her breasts. 'The trouble is,' he whispered to her, 'the you I'm in love with isn't the you you're in love with.' She squeezed him more tightly to her, and said nothing. 'But I don't believe Martin is in love with your you, either,' he added. 'I know you say he gives you amazing insights into yourself. As far as I can tell, he's just another CP member, the Compulsive Philanderers.'

'You may be right,' Lise whispered. 'I'm not sure myself. But it doesn't make any difference, whatever the truth is about Martin and me. He needs Sybil, and always will do. I could spend my whole life waiting for him. I may even do that. I've been ill with waiting for him, already. But I know he'll never leave her for me.'

'If you do that, you're wasting your sweet life, telling yourself a story that you can't even believe in.'

'But it's the best story I've got.'

'I'll give you a better one.'

'Will you, sweetheart?'

'Don't you believe me? Can't you?'

'I don't know.'

'That means, maybe you'll let me try?'

'It means I don't know.' She kissed him gently on the lips. 'This isn't the right time to know anything, when I'm likely to get shot by that psychopathic friend of yours, upstairs.'

'He won't shoot you. It's only blanks in the gun.'

'Oh no it's not. You're wrong. When you were out in the kitchen, he took the blanks out and put live ones in. He showed me them, just so that I'd know.'

'I don't believe it,' Andrew whispered.

'Take a look.'

He took the gun from where it lay across Willie. As his

151

fingers relinquished it, Willie stirred. Andrew waited, and Willie snuggled down in the armchair, without waking. Andrew broke the gun open, and saw that Lise was right.

'You see,' she whispered. 'Who are these people, Andrew?'

'I hardly know. I've lived in the same house as them, shared food with them, talked to them for hours, often about myself, and not once have they ever really told me anything about who they are. Ideas, dreams, are what they gave me in return.'

'Yet you brought them here.'

'It's another dream of theirs. All their ideas fit together, not like mine. But the cartridges weren't live, not till now.' He looked at them, in his hand. 'That wasn't the plan.'

'What was the plan?'

'A guerrilla raid on your father's brains, they called it. They were going to try him, while you and your mother watched. Then the punishment was to slip him a dose of LSD.'

'And then?'

'That was it. Not this.' Andrew drank some cognac from the bottle. 'I said okay to that. Why shouldn't I, after what he's done to me?'

'What are you going to do now?'

He swigged some more cognac, and said, 'I'll get you out of here. Where are your clothes?'

'The other one took them with him, upstairs.'

'Aren't there any more you could use, somewhere?'

'He's taken the coats, as well. But I did notice my bathrobe is still hanging inside the bathroom door.'

'Right.' Andrew put the cartridges in his trousers pocket, clicked the gun shut, and laid it back across Willie. He pulled his half-mask down over his nose again. As Lise stood up, she gave him a kiss on his mouth, beneath the snout. He held her for a moment, looking into her eyes, reading in them what he wanted to. So be it.

Every tread of the old stairs creaked under their tiptoes. The bathroom door squeaked on its hinge, as Andrew shut it behind them. Lise was putting the bathrobe on when they heard steps outside, on the landing, and Julian asking, 'Who's that? Andrew?'

Andrew leaned against the door, and called, 'Hold on.' To Lise he whispered, 'Flush the toilet.' She did so. He beckoned her to him, and whispered close to her ear, 'I'll stall him. Lock the door after me, when you hear me coughing. Then get out of that window. It's only a short jump to the hillside. Ring your parents from the box down the road, and tell them to meet you somewhere else, not here. But don't say why. And don't ring the police, or I'll be in it with them.'

As he joined Julian on the landing, he was glad of the pig face over his eyes. He coughed, to cover the sound of the key turning behind him and to give himself time to think. 'I was exercising my marital rights,' he told Julian. 'I fancied it in the bath. She's just cleaning herself up. I'll bring her down again, when she's through.'

'How did she take it?' Julian asked, going downstairs.

'They're very tough, the upper class,' Andrew said.

'You'll be ready for your kip, then. The bed's warm for you.'

'No, I'll join you down there. I could do with a drop more of m'lud's cognac, to see the dawn in.'

Julian went into the drawing-room. Andrew banged on the bathroom door, and shouted, 'Come on, my lovely. I can look inside your head. You've got nothing to hide.' He touched his lips, where she had given him her kiss. 'Then go and forget me for ever,' he sang in a whisper to himself.

Downstairs, he could hear Julian waking Willie up. 'I should have brought some bennies for you,' Julian was saying, and Willie was giggling, drunk, and honking. Andrew stood on, sentry to a vacated bathroom, for another ten minutes. Now and then he shouted to Lise to

153

hurry up, and banged the door.

When he was sure, he walked down to the drawing-room. The stink of cognac came out to meet him. Willie was lying flat out on the chesterfield, smiling under his snout, an empty bottle in his hand, its contents spilled beside him, and dripping on to the carpet. Julian was leaning over him, stroking his hair, talking quietly.

Andrew picked up the gun where Willie had left it in the armchair. He crossed to the far end of the room, and stood in the corner by the window, holding the gun at port-arms. Julian looked up through his half-mask. 'Where is she?'

'She's gone. Fifteen minutes ago. We'll never catch her now.'

'You let her go.'

'Yes.'

'Willie,' Julian said, 'come on, sweetheart, we've got to go.'

'Why?' Willie asked.

'Andrew—' Julian looked up at him again, '—Andrew has changed his mind.'

Bad-Feet Willie sat up, and peered at the dark figure outlined against the dawning windows. 'Hey,' he said, 'he's got the gun.'

'It's all right,' Andrew said, bringing the gun to bear on them. 'It's only blanks. Both barrels.'

'Andrew,' Willie said, 'don't shoot, we are going.'

'Whether the retreat will be bloodless, however, is another question.'

'Come on, Willie,' Julian urged him, quietly. Willie was sobbing: fear played a part, and drink, and perhaps disappointment at missing the chance to find Justice deWitt guilty, but Andrew was sure that most of Willie's tears welled from a betrayed friendship.'

'Goodbye, Andrew,' they both said. He nodded. Willie

154

leaned on Julian to eke out his feet, as they left the house, and passed the window where Andrew stood, their wigs awry in the morning.

Andrew put the gun down, and sat on the chesterfield. The daylight hurt his eyes, through the piggy holes. His body sagged with exhaustion, but his mind was feverishly awake, dancing around Lise. He took a cigar from a silver box, lit it, and drew the smoke down deeply. His arms were limp beside him, and after a while the tip of the cigar, touching the cognac-drenched fabric of the chesterfield, set it smouldering, then alight, in little purple flames. When he saw what he had done, he didn't move, but watched the fire gather strength. 'That's it,' he said, and drew on the cigar again. 'Let them get on with it. Here comes the sun. It's all right.'

The puddle of cognac on the carpet had caught now, and from it the fire spread quickly through to the polyurethane gloss, across to the curtains, the escritoire, the oil painting, the ceiling. Tongues of flame descended through the air. Andrew, curled up on the blazing chester-field, used his last gasps of oxygen to laugh. Then the flames exploded the cartridges in his trousers pocket, by his head.

At whose fiction was he laughing, as he entered the fourth stage of the Bardo Plane, where he would receive the final judgment, from himself? We cannot follow him there. Perhaps he didn't laugh any more, when he reached the end of his idea, and judged it. Perhaps not. But isn't it pretty to think so?

The line of smoke from the deWitts' blazing thatch rose up nearly straight, chalking the blue sky in the early morning.

Three

ROLL CREDITS

'Fine,' said the producer, 'just fine. I like it a lot. I really do.'

Christow, 1975